Mislaid Love
AND
Found Bodies

MJ MILLER

TRADEMARK ACKNOWLEDGEMENTS

- Mighty Mouse Public Domain
- The Money Pit Amblin Entertainment
- Sherlock Conan Doyle Estate Ltd
- Watson Conan Doyle Estate Ltd
- Kemosabe NBC Universal
- The Raskins
- Alfa and Alfetta Fiat Chrysler Automobiles
- Dwayne "The Rock" Johnson
- Hocus Pocus Walt Disney Pictures
- Ricky Ricardo
- Gloria Estefan
- Rod Stewart
- Do you think I'm sexy (song title). Rod Stewart, Carmine Appice, Duane Hitchings
- NikonMitsubishi Companies
- Wi-FiWiFi Alliance
- BluetoothNot owned by a single entity
- AirstreamAirstream Inc
- It's My Life Bon Jovi Productions, Inc
- Indian Matchmaking Netflix
- Frankenstein Mary Shelley
- NetflixCompany name
- Doctor Dolittle Public Domain
- CSIParamount Global (tv series only)
- Red Bull Red Bull GmbH
- Yelp YELP

- Coca-Cola Coca-Cola Co.
- Go-Go's
- Helen Reddy
- I am woman (song title)Helen Reddy, Capital Records
- An Officer and a Gentleman Paramount Pictures
- Richard Gere
- When Harry Met Sally Columbia Pictures
- Bridget Jones Universal Pictures
- Marilyn Monroe
- Casanova
- InstagramMeta
- Alice Cooper
- Tony Bennett
- JeepFiat Chrysler
- Airstream ©2007-2022 Airstream, Inc. | a subsidiary of Thor Industries, Inc.
- Frederick Lynn, Chicago Store privately owned by Aaron Comes
- GoogleAlphabet Inc
- Sharpie – Newell Brands
- Evel Knievel
- Glinda from The Wonderful Wizard of Oz (1900) L. Frank Baum public domain
- Bon Jovi's Always Lyrics: Bon Jovi Sung by: Bon Jovi produced by Polygram
- Jon Bon Jovi

CHAPTER ONE

Babs: Pippa! Emergency! Get over to the money pit, now!

I stared at the text and groaned. Not just because my twin sister had ruined my perfect moment with Devon and me under the spectacular midnight blue Colorado sky that twinkled with stars, but because the money pit she referred to was my future home. The house was part of an old estate purchased as a gift by my mother and her BFFs—Luckland's finest crew of rabble-rousers.

"What is it?" Devon asked. He cocked his head and squinted. With a lock of his thick, wavy hair dangling in front of one eye, the man was incredibly adorable.

"Babs. She says there's an emergency at our very own Mystic Manor." I sighed as I texted back a reply, though I doubted it was a real emergency, especially because, as chief of police, Devon would have received a text of his own.

"Well, Red, I guess we'd better be off then," he said.

I used to reflexively kick back at Devon calling me Red, which referred to my mop of red curls, though his nickname was growing on me.

"But first…" He leaned over and kissed me. Long and slow. A kiss I felt all the way down to my toes.

"Well done, Casanova, but we'll never get anywhere if you keep that up," I said when I caught my breath. Laughing, he stood, grabbed my hand, and pulled me up.

Luckland wasn't a large town, so it didn't take long for us to reach the Manor. Babs's car, as well as a few SUVs, stood out front.

We pulled up, got out, and headed to the entrance of our old gothic stone structure, which was under renovation. The door stood wide open.

"Should we go in?" I whispered as I held Devon's hand.

"No time like the present," he whispered back, giving my hand a reassuring squeeze.

We stepped inside the large foyer and, following a cacophony of voices, immediately headed up the frayed, red-carpeted stairs.

The master bedroom suite was in total disarray. Since that particular room required some major updates, we had decided to begin the reno there, and the construction crew had pretty much ripped it down to the studs. Moonlight streamed through the windows, shining a silvery beam on the Luckland Ladies.

I had several names for the ladies, none less descriptive of the mayhem they caused wherever they went, but they consisted of my mom, Kate, along with Devon's mom, Matilda, and the remaining members of their tight-knit posse, Prudence, Hope, and her fiancée Marcy, who all talked at once.

Babs and her husband, Tom, who happened to be the architect in charge of this project, stood quietly by, but Leah, my three-year-old niece, sat upon Tom's shoulders with a bicycle helmet on her head, singing some gibberish that resembled one of her cartoon favorites.

Devon straightened his shoulders and held up his hand for

silence, which basically had no effect. It very rarely had before, so I wasn't surprised it didn't now. He turned to me, his new investigator-in-training since the start of some recent odd mysteries, and nodded. I gave one of my ear-piercing whistles. It did the trick every time.

"Babs, care to tell us what's happening?" Devon asked in the ensuing silence.

"Not a clue. We just got here. Something about strange noises though." She shrugged, helpful, as always. She might be my twin, but we were as fraternal as fraternal twins could be. She was little miss perfect. I was the firecracker.

"I see," said Devon. "Well then, Mom, care to explain?"

"The house needs to be cleansed," she announced, her tone unequivocal.

"It's under construction. Cleaning the house is not an emergency." He looked bewildered. Matilda had that effect on people. She was eccentric and full of surprises. I couldn't anticipate what she'd say or do next. Ever.

"Not cleaned, dear boy, *cleansed!*" she replied as if her explanation was perfectly sensible.

"I think she's talking about smudging again, Dev," I said. Matilda had begun to explore her intuitive side—with a little help from ghost-hunting cable channels.

"Quite right, Pippa," said Prudence. "Tillie has been sensing some very strange goings on, and after the basement incident, we thought it important to investigate."

That was when I began to see some light. One of Prudence's exes had recently tried to blow up her basement, which put the ladies on high alert. I gave Devon a sidelong glance—my hint that he should remain quiet because I was sure more information would follow.

"It *is* October, exactly the time of year to expect oddities," Hope said. Hope was an aspiring playwright, an avid reader, and a former librarian. "Not surprising at all that we heard what we heard."

Devon shook his head, but before he had a chance to say something, my mom spoke up.

"The emergency, Devon, is that something is making a horrifying noise when clearly there should be total silence in here."

Now we were getting somewhere.

"What kind of noise, Mom?" I asked. "I don't hear anything odd. Seems pretty quiet."

My mom held up her hand and looked about. "Shhh. Everyone be quiet for a moment. Listen."

Everyone held their breath, eyes wide as if that allowed them to hear better, and waited. Nothing.

"I'm afraid I don't hear anything," said Devon, using his authoritarian voice, which had about as much effect as holding up his hand.

"Keep listening, my boy," said Matilda. "I promise you'll hear it."

Devon sighed and glanced at me, but he acquiesced. We all repeated the wide-eyed breath-holding ritual—except Leah, who decided to start singing again. Tom took that as his opportunity to make a speedy exit. Coward that he was. Maybe that was harsh, but I was just a wee bit jealous he was allowed to jump ship.

I waited with bated breath, expecting some sort of clanking like old pipes or something, but what broke the silence sounded as if someone had stepped on a cat's tail. Not that I'd ever done so, but I'd seen plenty of viral videos. Maybe there was a feral feline in the attic. I figured I'd let them all speak their mind before I mentioned my sensible and plausible suggestion.

The high priestesses of small-town living stood almost in a huddle and held one another's hands, all looking quite determined as if they were on trial. Melodramatic, as always—right down to their attire. Because it was close to Halloween, I shouldn't have been surprised they were costumed up, but they'd all dressed alike in black leggings and black long-sleeve tops, which did surprise me. If they'd been strangers, they might have been mistaken for cat burglars.

Matilda stepped forward, clearly taking the lead. She stood tall and proud—her usual stance when caught in an awkward situation. She was quite striking, with her cap of ebony hair and fiery blue eyes.

"I assume you two heard that?" She looked from Devon to me and back again. "That is not normal, as I'm sure you'd agree. It's an omen." She glanced at her comrades, who all nodded.

"An omen. I see," said Devon, nodding as if agreeing. "May I inquire as to what you think this is an omen of?"

The women all began chattering at once, offering up a bizarre round-robin of answers, which prompted Devon to hold up one hand in an effort to silence them, then two hands. Finally, he snapped.

"For god's sake, ladies, one at a time!"

That certainly had an impact. I smiled at him, proud he was finally getting the hang of keeping order among the posse.

Babs cleared her throat. "I'm going out on a limb here, but that, most definitely, was a cat. I know that sound."

I blinked. Babs coming forward and saying something while in the middle of the chattering ladies was a rarity, but when she did involve herself, she was most definitely the calm in the center of a Luckland storm. Not because she had some sort of inner serenity—she just wasn't interested in being a problem solver. She focused on herself, her family, and her daily routine. That was about it. So, what made her announcement even more astonishing was that she'd thought what I'd thought. I guess that boded well for me.

"Leah often, accidentally, of course, trips over Fester. That is the sound he makes," she said.

I nodded. "I thought the same thing, though not from first-hand experience."

Babs sidled over to stand next to me, which was an act of bonding and our wall of defense because we knew what we were about to encounter.

"Girls, that is not a cat," said our mother, her expression haughty. "Not even close."

"How about we all reconvene this discussion outside," said Devon. It seemed he'd had enough and wanted the women out of the house.

I'd taken a step to head down the stairs when the floors and walls suddenly shook, and something, be it cat or evil creature from hell, went careening through the air and out the bedroom window, shattering the glass.

CHAPTER TWO

The next few minutes were like a scene from a teen horror movie. Instead of the teen screamers, however, the group running out the door was a horde of sixty-year-olds, followed by three thirty-year-olds, one of whom, I was sure, wished he'd stayed at home. In any case, we all ended up out front.

"What was that?" I asked no one in particular.

Devon turned to me. "I'll go and check. You and everyone else stay here."

I wasn't going anywhere, but I was curious to know what my mother and her band of friends were doing at my house in the first place.

I grabbed my sister's arm and directed her to the curb, where I pulled her down to sit next to me. The women stood smack dab in the middle of the front yard, all talking at once, their tone hushed so we couldn't hear a word.

I turned to Babs. "Okay, want to tell me what everyone was doing in the house?"

"Honestly, Pip, I have no idea. Mom texted me to come over, so I did. I don't know what they were up to."

I didn't think the women knew what they were up to half

the time, but there was always something going on with them. Figuring out what that might be was the challenge.

"All right, I'm going to go ask. See what I can find out."

I stood, brushed off the dust on my jeans, then headed over to the women. "Mom?"

"Yes, Pip, what is it?" She acted as if standing in the middle of my yard after running out of my house because something creepy happened in there was a perfectly normal situation, which, considering what we'd all gone through the last few months, probably was.

"Why are you all here?" I asked.

"Because we were attacked by a flying creature, Pippa. Why else?"

"No. Mom. What were you all doing in my house?" I'd learned early on that the first rule with the Luckland Ladies was to be direct.

"What do you mean?" she asked. "Where should we have been?"

"I don't know. Your house? Tillie's? Pru's? Anywhere but *my* house."

"Technically, dear, it's not quite yours yet."

"Well, that's a low blow, Mom. Are you taking back your gift?"

"Don't be silly. I don't know what's gotten into you. We came over because we were planning a sur..."

"Don't say it, do not say that word." If there was one thing in this world I detested, loathed, and was unable to cope with, it was a surprise. Nobody was allowed to surprise me. Nobody —unless it was so fabulous, I made an exception. Like when Devon bought me an antique locket at a yard sale. That was an acceptable surprise. Otherwise, surprises were a phobia of mine. I liked to know exactly what was happening. Probably because growing up in Luckland, there was a never-ending supply of surprises. Nothing was ever as it seemed.

"We had a lovely idea for the master suite, and we just wanted to take a look at the progress and figure out a few things, that's all," she said. "Neither here nor there at this point. It seems there are bigger issues at play."

"The flying creature?"

"Of course. We must find out what it was."

"*We* don't need to do anything. Let Devon handle it."

After a non-verbal conversation with her friends, where they just looked at one another, my mom nodded. "Fine, we'll go. Did you want a ride, or will you wait for Devon?"

"I'll wait, of course." I wasn't really keen on waiting in the dark while he searched the yard for some poor dead critter, but it beat the alternative. After everyone had gone, including Babs, I sat back down on the curb, then quickly stood again, trying not to imagine what might be scurrying around the yard, or worse, and wishing I'd taken that ride.

"Boo!"

I think I jumped six feet in the air.

"That was so not funny," I said once my heart stopped racing.

Devon grinned. "I couldn't resist."

Some things would never change. Tormenting me was one of them. Devon was not a particular favorite of mine growing up. He was annoying, a complete nerd, and my chief persecutor, constantly tugging on my pigtails and leaving little creatures in my lunch bag. Then, a few months ago, he'd returned to Luckland, all grown up. *My* grown-up self soon recognized that all the friction between us had miraculously transformed into something far more electric. We were still working out the kinks though.

He grabbed me around the waist and drew me in for a kiss, quickly erasing all memories of mischief.

"Did you find the catapulting creature?" I asked once I'd gotten my breath back.

"No. I think we'll have Tom send some of the crew to look around tomorrow and see if there's some sort of nest in the walls or something."

I considered that for a moment. The idea creatures might have a nest in the walls of my future home did not sit well. "Perhaps it would make more sense to call an exterminator."

"Clearly, Red, the crew ought to be able to find any unwanted creatures."

"Clearly, that's ridiculous, Mighty Mouse. They're carpenters and construction experts, not rodent control."

"Nevertheless, I've already called Tom."

"Then this is an after-the-fact argument?" I was a little peeved at that.

"Of course. But that means we get to have an after-the-completely-unnecessary-argument make up session, right?" His eyes glinted with mischief. I should have huffed off in righteous indignation, but I didn't. I was only human. Instead, I sighed and allowed him to pick me up and carry me off to the car. It was totally worth it.

We arrived back at the Manor the following morning, greeted by a crew of workers scurrying about the front lawn—or what would someday be a lawn, planting little stakes with orange flags everywhere. Tom stood on the concrete and stone porch, apparently directing the tradesmen.

We weren't even close to doing any sewer or pipe work yet,

so I had no idea what they were up to. We headed over to where Tom now conferred with a helmeted crewmember.

"Tom, what's all this?" asked Devon.

Tom's expression showed a little consternation as if he hadn't expected us to be there. "Ah, well. We're digging up the yard."

I took another look at the crew, who had all stopped what they were doing and were listening to our conversation.

Devon frowned. "I asked you to find a den of critters in the walls of the house. I didn't ask you to start digging around our yard."

"That's true, Devon, and I apologize, but your mom kind of did." Tom then looked at me. "So did yours, along with the others, and since their names are still on the actual deed to this property, you'll have to take it up with them." He nodded toward the road.

I turned just as the ladies came barreling down the road in my mom's SUV. I squeezed Devon's hand. A silent reminder to put on his diplomatic hat.

"Ladies," he said as they approached, his tone pleasant. "Good morning to you all."

Well done.

"Now, Devon, we can explain." Matilda, knowing him best, probably saw right through his façade.

"Please, Mother, do explain," he replied, his tone now laced with humor, which was a good sign his anger had abated.

She waited for a moment, looking to make sure her partners in crime were by her side. "We were on our way home last night when we suddenly realized what had happened. My intuition was on high alert."

"Yes! As soon as Tillie said she knew, we all knew," exclaimed my mom while nodding emphatically.

"You have a ghost," Hope said.

"A ghost?" I shook my head before I glanced at Devon. He took a deep breath.

"Fine, we have a ghost. That doesn't mean you have to dig up our yard."

"Oh, well, it's the bones, you see. We have to find them."

Devon straightened his spine. "Human bones?"

"No, of course not. Don't be silly, Devon. It's obviously a cat or some other critter."

"So why do you have to find the bones?"

"We have to move them," Prudence declared. "The critter will continue to haunt you otherwise."

"So, you're digging up the yard to get rid of the ghost?" I asked. That was all utter bullshit. The ladies were up to something. Something elusive.

Devon must have also come to the same realization because he gazed at the posse, eyebrow raised. "We appreciate your concern. However, we don't want you digging up *our* front yard."

"Oh, well. Of course, it's your yard," my mother said. "But if we don't find the bones..."

"Leave them where they are," Devon said, voice firm. He turned to me, and it seemed the right time to make an exit.

As we headed toward the car, Devon grabbed my hand. "Is it me, or are they acting weirder than normal?"

"Weirder. Definitely weirder."

"Right. We need to keep a closer eye on them. Are you up for more investigative work, Red?"

I groaned because keeping an eye on the ladies usually spelled disaster.

CHAPTER THREE

"Oh. My. God."

I hadn't meant to say that out loud, but I must have.

"What?" Devon looked up from the stove. Usually, Mondays were kind of a slap-together whatever sort of meal day, but after finding out the women wanted to dig up our yard that morning, Devon decided to pamper me. One of the many wonders of Devon was his culinary ability. I had none. He could have had his own cooking show. Hell, he could have had his own cooking show even if he couldn't cook. He was *that* photogenic at well over six feet tall, with broad shoulders, a mop of chestnut hair, and the most exquisite aquamarine eyes I had ever seen. Standing there, spatula in hand, wearing those worn-out snug-fitting jeans and a rib-hugging t-shirt, he was quite delicious.

"The Raskins are going to be in Denver," I said.

"And?"

I sometimes forgot he was a country twangy fan and not into the rock scene at all.

"And we should go. They're awesome."

"Unless it's Keith or Toby, I can't really see that happening."

"What if the opening act was Trey Marks?"

Now that got his attention.

"Bring it here. I can't leave the mushrooms, or they'll burn."

I showed him my phone.

He read the information on the screen out loud. "Special guest, Trey Marks. Well, I'll be damned. We have to go."

It wasn't a coincidence that Trey Marks and Devon Marks shared the same last name. More of an accident at birth—or an accidental birth. One starry night in Vegas about thirty years ago, Trey performed a Bon Jovi tribute at one of the casino nightclubs. The Luckland Ladies were celebrating my mom's forthcoming nuptials. Trey and Matilda locked eyes, then locked lips, then, well, nature took over. When she discovered she was pregnant, she decided not to look him up. Not to tell him. In fact, she never told Devon. Instead, she raised him as her nephew following the kidnapping of her fictional sister in the Congo.

Quite recently, Devon learned the truth, and it appeared he was ready to face his heritage.

"I'm on it, Kemosabe. Maybe Dani can come," I said.

"Maybe Simon too?" Simon was Devon's old FBI pal, and Dani was my lifelong BFF. They'd met recently, and the sparks that flew could have started a ten-thousand-acre wildfire.

I grinned, then sobered. "Are you going to tell your mom?" Telling her might be tricky.

"No, I don't think so. I think we should just go and assess the situation. You know if I tell her, they'll all board that RV and show up unannounced." He laughed and shook his head.

"Not a good idea, I get it. Okay, four tickets it is." I submitted my request and waited for the confirmation email. Then I forwarded it to Dani with a message.

Me: You, me, Devon, and Simon.

She sent me an emoji back with the shades. The trip was

going to be awesome. I couldn't wait. I just had to contain my excitement and keep it secret. I was terrible with secrets. Secrets and surprises were my downfall and the bane of my existence. I was working on changing that though.

Tuesday flew by without a hitch. There was no more digging or shenanigans at the Manor, and I found some time to work on an article for Nature's Future, an online organization dedicated to climate change education. My sideline, when not working at the family antique store, was outdoor photography blogging, which landed me a recent gig on climate change with Nature's Future. This was my second project for them. I still wanted to pursue a career in outdoor photojournalism, but recent events had distracted me, like lost shoeboxes, threatening postcards, possible blackmail, kidnapping, murder, and general mayhem.

Devon had gone off to Denver for some secretive overnight mission. He mentioned Simon and an old case, which I thought was a cover for something else entirely. Devon had many secrets. Some he was willing to share with me, others not so much.

On Wednesday, I headed to my paid job at the shop. The delivery due that day was supposed to be just a handful of furniture pieces, so going in early meant I could help unload, do inventory, and be done by noon. However, when the semi-trailer arrived, and the driver handed over the bill of lading, it looked as if we'd acquired an entire household's estate.

"I'm sorry, but this must be a mistake. This is way more than we're expecting," I told the driver. He opened the back door of the trailer to show me.

I promptly grabbed my phone and called my mom. "We've

just received the delivery we expected today. Did you know how much you bought?"

"Well, no. But it's the second lot," she replied as if that explained it all.

"What second lot?"

"Nadia McConnell's. You remember, I only bought the first lot, but Nate, the auctioneer, told me the second lot wasn't sold, so he offered it to me, and as Nadia is related to me, I couldn't really refuse, could I?"

"They won't fit in the shop, you know. We'll need to store some of this elsewhere for now."

"All right, I'll grab your father, and we'll be right over."

That was not as simple as it sounded as they didn't live in the same house. Instead, they lived next door to each other, mainly because my dad couldn't live with my mom's clutter. Despite that, I hoped they'd hurry as I was stuck trying to figure out where everything would go.

After heading off to the bakery and returning with a really tantalizing bribe of freshly baked banana muffins and some fairly superb coffee, I sat and made small talk with the driver. Turned out that Rusty, the driver, was highly susceptible to bribes. Usually, these guys were in such a hurry they practically dumped the pieces on the sidewalk. By the time my mom and dad pulled up, Rusty was comfortably ensconced in one of the leather wingback chairs in the back of the truck, perfectly content, enjoying his treats.

My dad stood at the rear of the truck, and hands on hips shook his head. My mom stopped next to him, peered into the truck, then, with *her* hands on hips, also shook her head. They made quite the pair. With his thick mop of red hair and full beard, he stood over a foot taller than my tiny little mom with her blonde bob.

"Aren't either of you going to say anything?" Did they think I was somehow going to deal with this? Not likely.

"Looks as if we'll have to use the barn," said my mom.

"Quite right, Katie," said my dad.

"What barn?" I raised my eyebrows at my parents.

They looked at each other, then back at me—clearly not a good sign. I stared them down, hoping to elicit some sort of response.

"Perhaps your dad should show you," my mother said.

The driver had polished off the box of muffins by then and was clearly ready to unload, as evidenced by his pacing outside the truck.

My father approached Rusty and, after a brief confab, came back over and said we were all set. Rusty would follow us to the barn. I hopped into the passenger seat of my dad's pickup, then we headed out to points unknown, to me at least.

We'd only traveled about ten miles out of town when realization dawned.

"Dad, this is the way to the cabin, is it not?"

"'Fraid so, Punkin."

"The cabin doesn't have a barn," I said with a great deal of suspicion. The cabin was a co-owned venture of the Luckland Ladies. Many years ago, after stumbling across a bag full of stolen casino cash, they built the little palace in the mountains as a place for them to unwind. Growing up, it was also a sanctuary for Babs, Devon, Dani, and me.

As palatial as the cabin was, it didn't have a barn. I knew that for a fact.

"Can you keep a secret?" my dad asked.

"No, you are quite aware I can't."

"You'll have to try for me, sweetheart, okay?" He patted my knee as if that would assure him of my confidentiality. Ha!

"Can I tell Devon?" I asked because who else would I tell? Except maybe Dani. Or Babs.

"Okay. Otherwise, I'll know you'll burst." He laughed as he said that. When my dad laughed, he sounded like Santa Claus. Hard to resist laughing with him.

As we approached the turnoff we normally took for the cabin, we continued straight for another mile or so. There was no street sign, no indication of any kind that there was a secret road anywhere between the dense cropping of pine trees.

"Okay, how come we've never come up this way before?"

"I suppose we've never had occasion to, Pip," my dad answered somewhat blithely.

"Not good enough, Dad. Let's try that again, shall we?" I'd recently learned I wouldn't get any answers if I didn't ask the right questions. Devon said it was the first rule of investigation.

"Because the barn has a few items stored there that are, shall we say, not for public viewing."

What an odd remark, especially from a man who had an alien gnome on his workbench not long ago.

"Okay, Dad, I'll bite. What kind of items?"

"Almost there, Pip, and you can see for yourself."

We approached a clearing, which was more of a plateau, common on the eastern slopes of the Rockies. Smack dab in the middle sat an enormous, weathered barn surrounded by a meadow filled with wildflowers. The barn itself—an old, high-pitched gable style, intrigued the photographer in me. I could capture its essence and use it as a great backdrop. However, I didn't have my camera, and my phone had only twenty percent charge left. After leaving it plugged in to charge all night, I awoke to discover the charger itself wasn't connected to the wall. Most likely, 99, my white ball of feline fur, had played with the cord.

We approached the giant barn doors, and each of us took

hold of one door and swung it open. Thankfully, I was in fairly good shape from hiking and the occasional attempt at some sort of weight, or weightless, training. Those doors were monsters. Stepping into the entryway, I really didn't know what to expect. Stacks of hay, maybe? Some horse stalls? Old rusted-out farm implements?

Certainly *not* a matching pair of Formula One race cars.

CHAPTER FOUR

"Are those real?" I asked after recovering from the shock. I'd never seen a Formula One car up close and personal. Or from afar. Closest I'd been to one was when my dad watched a race on TV. He was a big fan.

He grinned. "You betcha!"

"There's a story behind this, isn't there?" I asked, knowing full well it would be a doozy. I didn't know much about race cars, but I did know they were expensive. Very, very expensive. I also knew there weren't any race car drivers in our family. Or circle of friends.

I sighed. "Since Rusty is pulling in now, I don't think you have time to explain. Shouldn't we cover them up?" I pointed to the bin of tarps nearby, wondering why the cars weren't already covered. Someone had to have been here recently. Very recently. We quickly covered the cars, and just in time as Rusty headed our way.

We showed him where everything would go, and even with our help, it took a good hour and a half. When Rusty left, I still faced inventorying the enormous load.

"Okay, Dad, spill it. We'll be here for a while as I need to get these pieces checked over, so start talking."

"Well, not much to tell. They belonged to Elvis."

"What?" That was a bit far-fetched even for my dad.

"Oh, not that Elvis, my Uncle Elvis, though really his name was Timothy. He was an Elvis impersonator."

"You're just telling me this now? That your uncle was an Elvis impersonator who owned a couple of race cars? You know that sounds crazy, right?" I knew there was more to the story. My dad didn't talk about his family much. My grandmother died when I was young, and my grandfather was absent from the picture altogether—he'd abandoned my grandmother and ran off with a Peruvian archaeologist when my dad was little. I only knew that much because my dad took me out on my twenty-first birthday for a "pint or two," but he had a bit more than that. Loose lips.

"You see, Uncle Elvis was my father's brother. They were quite different, obviously. When Dad took off, Elvis stepped in to try to help. He would send money when he could and came to visit pretty often. Well, on one such visit, he went to a local bar with a back room."

"Back room?"

"Poker, in the back, totally illegal but common. One of the gentlemen playing was losing badly and made a crazy bet. He said he had a pair of race cars and put an IOU for them in the pile. He lost. Elvis won. Sure enough, several days later, these beauties arrived! At the time, we simply put them in the garage out back. Elvis said they'd be safe there as nobody would ever suspect something of this value in our neighborhood."

"So, these cars are like fifty years old?"

"Older than that. They were from the very first racing season, in 1950."

"But they look brand new!"

"They've been well cared for." Dad whisked off the tarps with a flourish, then lovingly ran a hand over the smooth rear curve of one of the cars. Both a glossy red, the one-seater sports cars were quite beautiful. Long, low, and sleek. I wondered what Devon would think. Maybe I wouldn't tell him. He'd want to drive them. No way was that happening.

"Have you ever driven them?"

"Perhaps I have, Pip, perhaps I have," Dad said with a twinkle in his eye. Because my dad resembled a cross between a giant teddy bear and a lumberjack, I didn't think he could fit in one of these beauties, but I wasn't going to ruin his story.

"Maybe I could drive one someday," I said hopefully. "You could teach me." Dropping a few hints couldn't hurt.

"I'll let Devon show you the ropes. My racing days are over."

"Devon! Devon already knows? How? Why?"

As my dad realized he'd let the cat out of the bag, he groaned. His verbal slip wasn't quite as bad as when he accidentally revealed Matilda was Devon's mother, but my dad knew he was in the doghouse. Clearly, I'd acquired my secret-keeping skills, or lack of them, from my dad, but I had no idea where I'd suddenly acquired my overuse of idioms.

"Sorry, Pippa, but when Devon got his learner's permit, Tillie asked me to teach him to drive. I felt if he could learn to drive one of these babies, he could drive anything."

"And yet you taught me to drive in the family sedan. I see. Was it because he was a boy? I must say I'm certainly disappointed in you!" I sounded like my mother.

"Oh, Punkin, it wasn't you. It was Babs. She would never have been able to handle it. I couldn't very well bring you out here and leave her behind, now, could I?"

"Why yes, yes you could." I sighed. "Is Devon aware I didn't know about the barn or the cars?"

"I did swear him to secrecy. It was one of our pacts."

"*One* of your pacts? There were others?"

"Oh dear. I should quit while I'm ahead!"

I considered whether to text Devon with my newfound knowledge but decided not to. I'd wait until he got home. Then I realized I couldn't hold out that long.

Me: Guess where I am?

Devon: Where?

Me: Guess?

Devon: Lying naked in the bed, waiting for me?

I had to smile at that, but only for a moment.

Me: The BARN!

That ought to make him realize the seriousness of the situation.

Devon: Oh. I see. I should probably head home then.

Me: Why yes, you probably should.

Devon: Will you be lying naked in the bed?

It was so hard to stay mad at him, but I had to do my best to try.

First things first, however, I had a truckload of relics to inventory. I surveyed the new items that Rusty had placed neatly along the far side of the barn. They took up about a third of the space, which was quite a bit. It was a very ordinary-looking lot though. Nothing jumped out at me as being unique or particularly old. I glanced at my dad to see if any particular piece struck his fancy, but he seemed to have the same reaction I did. Meh. Maybe upon further inspection, we'd find a hidden gem. I could never tell. For now, we simply agreed to leave it all and come back and inspect it another day.

Just as we were closing the large barn doors, a flash of something caught my eye. I turned and frowned. Sitting at the base of a tree was an old man dressed in clothes that had to have come from the beginning of the previous century. In one hand, he held a knife. In the other, a small piece of wood. As I stared, he whittled the wood with the sharp edge of his blade, leaving shavings on the ground around his feet. As he caught me watching, he tipped his head and winked—just the way Devon did. Then he vanished. He didn't get up and walk away. He simply vanished. Gone. Evaporated.

"Dad?" Goose bumps peppered my skin as I grabbed his sleeve and pulled at him to get his attention. I pointed at the tree, my hand not quite shaking but close. "Did you see that?"

"What's that, Pippa? See what?"

"A man. There was a—" Was there though? Or was it all in my imagination?

Dad strode to where I pointed, and I slowly followed. There was nothing there. Not even shavings from the wood the man had been carving.

"Are you sure? It can't have been Rusty, he's long gone, and we would have heard another vehicle."

"I—" I shook my head. "I don't know. Perhaps it was a trick of the light."

"Or maybe one of Luckland's spirits," my dad said, his tone teasing.

"You don't believe in ghosts," I said, sure in my statement.

"Don't I? There are a lot of things that happen in Luckland that don't have many explanations. I don't see why we can't blame them on the ancestral spirits known to roam the town."

"That's just a legend to bring in the tourists like Luckland's gold." The recent influx of tourists for our Founders' Day celebration, where we handed out maps to "find" the gold, was a great revenue boost for the town, but the "ghosts" were an all-year-round phenomenon that brought in oddballs, most of whom stayed at our very own Luckland Inn, rumored to be haunted by the Scarlet Lady. Until recently, I hadn't believed there was gold in Luckland, but after certain events where Prudence's ex had murdered one of her other exes in order to find the gold, I'd begun to think maybe there was some truth behind the legend—and if I believed the gold could be real, maybe I shouldn't discount Luckland's legendary spirits.

"Is it though? Your mom and the other ladies do their yearly ritual to appease the spirits. If they don't do it, the spirits will rise. This year— Never mind. Just remember, not everything is as it seems."

With his sage advice ringing in my ears, we headed back to town in silence. He may have thought I was brooding because Devon knew about the cars and the barn. However, my thoughts were stuck on the old-timer. As a photographer, I considered myself quite observant, and I relied on that skill to capture moments with my camera. I'd trained myself to notice things and see them as they truly were, and if I hadn't seen a flesh and blood man vanish into thin air, what had I seen? Certainly not a trick of the light.

As it was almost lunchtime when we arrived back in Luckland, Dad pulled up in front of the Blue Sky Café. Hope and her fiancée Marcy owned this lovely little eatery, and the food was fabulous. As long as Morgan, the town flirt, wasn't around, it'd all be good.

CHAPTER FIVE

DAD AND I SAT AT A BACK TABLE AWAY FROM THE FAKE WEBS WITH giant rubber spiders dangling from the ceilings. The skeleton at the front door of the café was bad enough, but I was not fond of arachnids. Plus, Halloween decorations tended to bring out the worst of my fears. Whatever happened to simple pumpkins that didn't have blood dripping from their jaggedly cut mouths? The café's decorations were truly horrifying but spying Morgan in her witch's hat was what really set me on edge.

Morgan was an attention-seeking, flirtatious homewrecker who never quite understood when to stop and didn't care who she hurt in the process, but I generally ignored her behavior—until Devon came back to Luckland and she made it very clear she had her eye on him. I wasn't sure what she thought she would get from him, but she definitely wasn't getting it.

I shut her out of my mind and perused the menu but couldn't decide whether to have the truly spectacular lasagna or Marcy's Harvest Pie, an extraordinary, spiced apple concoction. Deciding on the pie and remembering my promise to the ladies, I grabbed my phone, ready to take a photo of the pie for the café's Instagram feed. Ever since someone had leaked Hope and Marcy's cheesecake and lasagna recipes online, I'd created a social media campaign to keep the café at the forefront of everyone's mind. We hadn't figured out who or why someone had leaked the recipes other than assuming they had one of the missing six shoeboxes, but as a result, café patrons had increased, and business had been better than ever.

"Boo!"

I jumped and looked up to find Devon grinning from ear to ear.

"Excuse me, Chief Pumpkin Patch, do you think it's appropriate for the local chief of police to be going around scaring the living daylights out of the locals?"

"Aren't you glad to see me?" he asked as if he hadn't just taken years off my life.

Devon leaned down and kissed me hello, an enormously public display in front of what amounted to the entire town. Then he pulled over a nearby chair, grabbed a menu, and acted as if kissing in public was perfectly normal.

I pulled my menu in front of my face to hide my grin, happy to have Devon at my side—until Morgan sidled up to him and placed her hand on his shoulder.

"What can I do for you, Chief?" she asked Devon, her voice all syrupy. It was pretty obvious she could take his order. Nothing more. My thirteen-year-old self wanted to toss a spitball her way. My sixteen-year-old self was ready to scratch her eyes out. My thirty-year-old self contemplated something unquestionably illegal, but I held myself in check.

"We don't know yet, Morgan. Can we call you back over when we're ready?" Devon asked, his tone neutral. He didn't like the way she flirted with him any more than I did.

She nodded and headed off to another table, and I breathed a little sigh of relief. Just as I was about to ask him how his trip to Denver went, the door to the café blew open, and in marched the high priestesses of Luckland. I was surprised the skeleton didn't keel over. They beelined it straight to the back, past our table, and through the swinging doors that led to the kitchen. All but one. Matilda wasn't with them. That was odd. I looked at Devon, and Devon looked at my dad. Clearly, some sort of ladies' auxiliary conference was going on back there. One that didn't involve Matilda. A familiar sensation at the back of my neck told me she was probably at the center of it all. The others had to be discussing her.

Devon glanced at me and tipped his head as if he knew what I was thinking. That was too terrifying a thought. Yes, we had a connection and were highly intuitive, but I truly didn't think mind-reading was one of his skills.

"What?" I stared back at him, trying to understand his weird expression.

"Are you thinking what I'm thinking?" he asked.

"I don't know. What are you thinking?"

My dad smirked as he glanced between Devon and me. "I'm thinking you two should work on your communication skills," he said, laughing.

"Thanks, Dad." That was just what I needed—relationship advice from Dad.

Devon began to rise out of his chair, but I grabbed a handful of his shirt to pull him back down. "You know you can't go in there."

A few minutes later, the posse marched out of the kitchen and right on out the front door as quickly as they had come in. Not so much as a hello. I wasn't sure the ladies even noticed we were there. I quickly rose to follow them out.

"Mom? Got a minute?"

She turned, and the others stopped alongside her.

"Of course, Pippa. What is it?"

"What are you up to?"

"Just making plans, dear," said Prudence, patting my arm for good measure.

"Yes, we're all headed to a show next week in Denver. That's all," said Hope.

"It's a bit of a surprise, so don't mention it to anyone, especially Matilda, okay?" My mom used her warning voice. Now that got my attention.

"Who are you seeing and when?"

Silence. My mom shifted her gaze toward her friends.

"Mom?"

"I'm sure you've never heard of them. A group out of L.A.," she replied.

Uh-oh.

"Well, we better be off. Tillie is waiting, and we have some errands to run." Prudence tugged at my mom's arm. Hope and Marcy quickly followed, all of them waving in the air as if they weren't leaving me hanging.

They'd said enough, however. They were going to see The Raskins with special guest Trey Marks. I saw a potential disaster in the making.

I hurried back inside. "Emergency. Impending doom," I said as I sat back down. Though my mom told me not to tell anyone, I'd learned my lesson where the ladies' secrets were concerned.

"I take it you've discovered the surprise," my dad said.

"You *knew*?"

He chuckled. "Of course I did. Nothing gets past me, you know."

"Who's going to fill me in?" Devon asked.

"We're not the only ones going to the concert," I replied.

The muscles in Devon's face twitched, and he narrowed his eyes. That was a look I hadn't seen before. He swung his gaze over to my dad. "You knew?"

"It'll be fine. Kate and the girls just wanted to go and enjoy the show."

"Dad, how do you not see a problem in all this?"

"I'm not sure I follow, Pippa. They have as much right to go to a concert as you do. They just didn't want anyone to know as it's a surprise for Tillie." He sat back and smiled as if what he'd said was obvious. I thought he was quite naïve.

"Colin, I'm curious. Do you know who they're going to see?" asked Devon, his face still one of consternation.

"Couple of guys out of L.A. I think they toured with Alice Cooper once. Or maybe it was Tony Bennett. I always confuse the two."

"They're going to The Raskins, Dad, and you know who the opening act is? Hmmm? Do you? Does the name Trey Marks ring a bell?"

His eyes widened. "Oh, dear."

Oh, dear, indeed.

CHAPTER SIX

"Make a list," Devon said as we drove home. "Number one, we have to find out why those women think taking my mom to see Trey Marks live in concert as a *surprise* is a good idea."

"True. I mean, what if she jumps up and yells, *'There's my baby's daddy?'*"

Devon glanced at me and narrowed his eyes. "Number two, why do the posse *really* want to dig up our front yard? I don't buy the bones thing."

"Number three, why you never told me about the barn." I had to add that for good measure, as I didn't want him to think he got away with it.

A mischievous grin spread across his face in response. He knew we'd discuss it. He also knew post-discussion he'd get lucky. That was how it usually worked between us, and I briefly wondered if he'd always known the extent of our chemistry. However, I wasn't letting him believe he'd get lucky this time. I crossed my arms over my chest.

He quickly removed the grin and cleared his throat. All business. "The barn. Okay. Your dad swore me to secrecy. That's it." He shrugged as if that explained it all.

"You were sixteen. Now you're not."

"A promise is a promise, Pip, don't you think?"

"Maybe, but keeping a secret from someone you're, let's say, sleeping with?" I realized then I might still have a few secrets I hadn't yet shared with him. Therefore, I should extricate myself from this conversation.

"On the other hand, I completely understand you were caught between a rock and a porcupine, and therefore, I forgive you. I do, however, expect you to teach me to drive one of those Alfas."

"Of course. If you're going to drive the *Alfetta*, though, you'll need to learn a bit about it first. Driving it requires knowledge and respect." His condescending guy voice was in place. I wasn't a fan.

"Alfetta? What is that? Your pet name for it?"

"That's the name of the model, Pip. Before I could drive it, your dad made me study everything about it, even the engine."

"Again, somehow, I knew none of this."

"You weren't really a classic car aficionado back then, were you? But if you're going to take a sudden interest in sports cars, you better be prepared to get your hands dirty."

I swore he sat a bit taller, shoulders back as he drove, suddenly filling *my* Jeep with testosterone. I seriously needed to nip that in the bud, and I would have had we not pulled into my driveway to find Dani on my front porch.

Devon hadn't even turned off the engine before I was out of the Jeep and leaping to greet my best friend. We had a thing we made up as kids. Two steps to the right. Two steps to the left. Shimmy down and shimmy up. Then we hugged. It had been over a month since I'd seen her last, but with her work as a deep-sea dive instructor, we didn't get to hang out too often.

Dani and I were quite alike, though not in appearance, of course. I was the quintessential redheaded green-eyed Irish girl while she was exotic and the product of a Dominican baseball player and a Cuban beauty. While puberty had been kinder to Dani than me, I believed I'd caught up in the end. At least Devon thought so. He said my emerald eyes were lethal weapons. He scored big points for that. Looks aside, Dani and I were the types of friends who finished each other's sentences, ate the same food, and drank the same wine.

We headed inside, then collapsed on the sofa in the family room, and I immediately started filling her in on the day's events. 99 planted herself between us, knowing she'd get attention from the two of us that way. Devon made himself busy in the kitchen, fixing lunch as we never got to eat, and I ceded all culinary tasks to him anyway.

"So. Tell me more about what's happening at the Manor. I talked to my mom this morning, and she said the oddest thing."

Dani's mom and dad retired to Tucson, but her mom Rosa was pretty much one of the posse and was always up on things.

"What did she say? About the Manor?"

The kitchen noises subsided. Devon was listening in. I smiled at Dani and nodded for her to continue as what she had to say also had to do with Devon.

"She said I should have you give me a tour of the place before it's all dug up."

A clang in the kitchen sounded as if Devon had slammed a pan on the stove. He'd clearly heard her.

"My *house*?"

"Correction, Pip," Devon called out. "*Our* house."

"Duly noted, Chief."

"Well, I'm not sure about the house, but according to my mom, the ladies wanted to do some excavation," Dani said.

I shook my head. "They said they needed to dig up some poor critter's bones, but I reckon that's an excuse for something else. We haven't got a clue what they're really doing."

"I wouldn't be surprised if they've suddenly decided to search for Luckland's gold," Devon remarked as he strode into our line of sight.

That actually made a lot of sense. On Founders' Day, after they'd done their customary "spirit-cleansing ritual," the ladies had followed gold prospectors around town and watched them like a hawk. I'd suggested to Devon that whatever secrets the women had in the lost shoeboxes might have had some information about the alleged gold. He'd agreed, but every time we tried to broach the subject with the posse, they shut us down.

"What would make them think it's in our yard?" I asked. "And why start digging there now?"

Devon shrugged. "Who knows what goes on inside their heads."

"Well, obviously, they couldn't dig beforehand because the house and land belonged to someone else," Dani said. "As the posse now technically own it, they probably thought it would be a good time to look for the gold."

I smiled because that also made sense, but I had a more pressing concern. "Unfortunately, we need to talk about the concert."

"Oh, don't tell me you can't go!"

"Oh, we're going, but guess who else is headed that way."

Realization dawned across Dani's face. "That explains why my mom said she was coming up for a visit. I just assumed it was someone's birthday or some such thing."

"My mom's," Devon said with a shake of his head. "Of course. It's my mom's birthday in a few days, so that's why the ladies are taking her to the concert. It's a birthday surprise."

"One that could end in another kind of surprise when Tillie and Trey come face to face, and Trey learns he has a son." I glanced at Devon as he bit his lower lip and grimaced.

I grimaced along with him. "Perhaps we shouldn't go."

"Don't worry, Pippa," Devon said quietly. Too quietly. "I know what to do."

We dropped the subject then, or rather he did as he busied himself getting food on the table. After lunch, Devon headed back to work, taking my Jeep as he'd left his hire car at the station. Dani and I used Dani's hire car and headed off to my favorite hiking trail, hopeful I might get a few photos taken after all.

Later that afternoon, as the sun began to set and the shadows of the pine trees gave off an ominous glow amid the darkening sky, I spotted my second apparition.

CHAPTER SEVEN

"Wʜᴀᴛ ᴛʜᴇ ʜᴇʟʟ?" I ғʀᴏᴢᴇ, ᴍʏ ɢᴀᴢᴇ ᴛʀᴀɴsғɪxᴇᴅ ᴏɴ ᴛʜᴇ ᴡᴏᴏᴅᴇᴅ area just beyond the horizon where a layer of fog slowly rose among the trees—and an apparition stood. Nothing like the man I saw earlier that day. This one was...spooky.

"What?" Dani asked.

"That," I whispered, still staring at the dissipating fog and the small figure now slowly moving toward us. "The *thing* coming out of the fog." I took a few steps back, trying to keep my distance. Dani stepped back with me, though her expression showed confusion and not caution.

"I don't see anything. Just trees."

I glanced at her. "Seriously? You don't see—" I turned to point, but where the fog had covered the ground, and the figure had stood, there were now...just trees. I shuddered, and it wasn't from the cool mountain air. "I think we need to go."

I headed for the trail that would take us back to the parking lot, Dani close on my heels.

"Pippa, what did you see?" She placed her hand on my arm, which steadied my nerves.

"A small figure. Not a child though. At the beginning of

summer, Devon saw a child while we drove back from the cabin early in the morning. At the time, Devon thought it was shadows from the trees or his overactive imagination. I agreed, but for a moment, I did wonder if any of Luckland's wayward spirits would be all the way up there."

"You don't believe in that legend, do you?"

"I didn't, but this isn't the first time I've seen something that shouldn't be there."

We reached Dani's hire car and hopped in. Dani started the engine and put the heater on full blast, which helped reduce the chill that still rode my spine.

"You know, when I'm diving, I see all kinds of things. I've had that experience before. Shadows and light can play some serious tricks. Might be all it was."

"No, because I also saw a man this morning." I took a deep breath, then described the apparition, how it had winked at me before vanishing, and how my dad suggested it was a spirit.

"Okay, that changes things, I guess, but I wouldn't worry about it. Neither of them seemed to want to do you harm."

I was sure she only said that to make me feel better, but she gnawed on her lower lip, deep in thought.

My Jeep was in the driveway when we got back, and I sighed in relief. I wanted to run my paranormal experience by Devon and see what he thought.

We found him relaxing on the sofa, 99 curled up on his chest. The house was noticeably absent of aromas, which meant dinner was not in progress. Though disappointed, seeing as Dani was there, we'd probably head over to the café.

"I can see you've taken the night off from culinary duties, so where shall we dine?" I asked ever so sweetly as I removed 99 from her suck-up position and carried her to the recliner.

"Clearly, Pip, our choices are limited in Luckland, so I suggest we head to the café." His reply was laced with humor. That was a good sign because it meant nothing terrible had happened in town that afternoon. We got the occasional vandal or vagrant, and perhaps a domestic spat every so often, but we lived in quite the crime-free community—apart from the crime spree we'd experienced over the summer. Those criminal transgressions were how Devon had landed the fabulous job of heading up the brand-new police department, the creation of which was the posse's doing. I didn't know the details, but I knew they were behind it. Financially at least. *How to keep Devon in Luckland? Hmm. Let's see. Maybe create the perfect job for him.* Typical posse move.

"I call dibs on lasagna if they're running low," Dani said, her head somewhere deep inside my fridge, looking for a cold beer, I supposed.

"Then we better get moving," Devon replied, jumping up off the couch. "They always run low."

I'd have hopped out of the chair myself, but 99 seemed to have other ideas. I silently begged Devon to remove her from my lap. If I were to try, she'd burrow with her claws, but she loved him so much she'd willingly go with him to the gates of hell if necessary. He brought her home one day, a gift for me after someone had ransacked my house, which had been part of the aforementioned crime spree. Turned out 99 was a bigger flirt than Morgan.

As the café was only a few blocks away, we decided to walk and take advantage of the rare, warm autumn night.

"Devon, remember that little illusion that stopped you cold on our way home from the cabin?" I asked.

"I'm not sure I'd use the term illusion, Red, but yes. I do recall the situation."

"Right. I had two of them today."

"She did, Dev. I was there for one of them," Dani said for good measure.

He stopped abruptly on the sidewalk and turned to me.

"What do you mean, you had two of those? You saw a child in the road? You were up by the cabin? I thought you were on a hike." So many questions and no time to answer.

"Yes, we were hiking, but that was when I saw the second apparition. The first one was this morning up at the barn."

"Explain," he said, crossing his arms over his chest.

"Okay, but can we keep walking, please. There's lasagna to be had." Funnily enough, being with Devon didn't make me fear what I'd seen. "So, this morning, I was with my dad, and while we were closing the barn doors, I saw an old man sitting at the base of a tree. He was whittling some wood, then when he caught me watching, he tipped his head and winked the same way you do. Then he vanished."

"He winked at you?"

"That's what you took from my tale?"

"Okay, so then he vanished. What then?"

"Dad said it could be a spirit." I wasn't sure what Devon would make of that, but he didn't bat an eyelash.

"And this afternoon on your hike?"

"Dani and I were in the meadow. I was looking over at the tree line, my camera shot lined up, and this bank of fog rolled in. Quite creepy. Then out of the fog, this darker shadow emerged, shaped like a small adult, and he or she carried something. Like a pickaxe. They also wore a helmet with a weird thing attached. Like a candle."

"A dwarf miner? Were they whistling a happy tune and singing hi-ho?" Devon chuckled, thinking he was quite clever.

"It isn't funny. I didn't laugh at your apparition. I'll kindly ask you to refrain from any mockery. It was quite terrifying."

His expression sobered. "Sorry, you're right, and I think we need to delve a little deeper into these apparitions. Odd as it may seem, you're not the only one who has seen such...visions. I've had several residents complaining they've seen things. At first, I'd put it down to a few too many beers or glasses of wine, but now I think there may be more to the mystical sightings."

Glad he was now taking me seriously, we continued to the café in contemplative silence, my thoughts centered on the ladies and their annual Founders' Day ritual. If the legend behind our ancestral spirits was real, and the women had completed the ritual as per usual, why were we now seeing ghosts?

***

The café was packed, as always. When there was only one eatery in town, it was expected. Worst case scenario, we could get our food to go, so coming here wasn't too big a risk.

We managed to find a table, and thankfully, I couldn't see Morgan anywhere. Instead, my favorite server, Finn McDougall, graced us with his presence A few years younger than me, he could charm the toes off just about anyone. Of course, his good looks, auburn hair, and green eyes didn't hurt. Between digs as an archaeologist, he came home and banked some funds for his next adventure.

"Hello, ladies, gentleman. What can I get you to drink," Finn asked, flashing a beautiful pearly white smile. "There's a fabulous batch of white sangria if you're interested."

"Most definitely interested, Finn," I replied with a smile of my own. More like a grin. He had that effect on people. Dani held up a finger and smiled, indicating she'd also have one. I glanced at Devon, who practically laughed out loud.

"Just a pint, Finn, thank you," Devon said, chuckling and shaking his head. I believed that was his way of silently signaling that Dani and I were a bit hopeless regarding Finn. I'd explained we were not Finn's type, as evidenced by his current boyfriend, but Finn was an exquisitely charming and beautiful man, and we could admire him in a "never-gonna-have-that" kind of way. At least Devon wasn't threatened by him.

As Finn went off to fetch the drinks, Devon pulled a slip of paper out of his pocket and unfolded it before smoothing out all the creases, so it lay flat. Then he put his hand over it.

"Know what I have here?" he asked, raising his brows and tipping his head.

Dani and I looked at each other and back at him.

"Nope," we said in unison.

He pushed the paper toward us, removed his hand, and leaned back, hands folded behind his head. That was known as the Devon Lean—a pose that seemed to ooze alpha male.

Dani and I quickly leaned forward to see what he'd found.

"Jon Bon Jovi?" I asked. "Back in the day?"

"Try again," Devon said. Well, if it wasn't Jon Bon Jovi, it could only be one person.

"Holy shinoozles!" Dani and I said in unison again.

"That's Trey, isn't it?" Dani asked.

"Clearly, Dani. I mean, look at this guy," I said.

The paper was a full-page photo printout of a guy who looked amazingly like the famous singer and, by extension, Devon. The picture showed Devon's father on stage, holding a microphone. The backdrop said Rocky Mountain Music 1993 on it.

"You know, it's quite possible that's the actual Jon Bon Jovi," I said because I just had to throw that out there.

"I googled the festival, Pip. That's a tribute act, Jon Von Jobi." Devon seemed amused rather than irritated. "Look again, though, closely." Devon had that curious tone in his voice. The one that meant he had something up his sleeve.

We examined the printout again. I saw it first and had to do a doubletake. I glanced at Dani, waiting for her to realize what she had seen, which didn't take her long.

We remained quiet as we looked at Devon for confirmation. I'd had my share of stunning revelations lately, but this one was over the top. The photo was taken at an angle. Probably from the side of the pit area in front of the stage. It captured Trey in action, mic in hand, along with some of the crowd rushing the stage. And there, in the first row, was a tall, striking young woman with a cap of ebony hair. It couldn't have been anyone but Matilda. Since she'd said she'd never attempted to see or contact Trey, as in *never*, seeing her in front of the stage was startling.

"What do you think? Do I say something?" Devon asked, his tone hesitant, though it was a good question.

"No," Dani said quite firmly. "There's a reason she didn't tell you. I can think of several. First, what if she tried to make contact, but he was with someone like a girlfriend or wife? Or, what if they made contact, and it didn't work out, and it isn't something she wants to remember?"

"All valid points, Dani," Devon replied with a sigh. "She'll tell me eventually, I'm sure."

I nodded. "Right, so for now, mum's the word." Though, as everyone knew, I was not good at keeping secrets. For Devon's sake, I was sure willing to try.

Devon suddenly snatched the paper away and shoved it in his pocket. Uh-oh—sure sign the ladies had arrived, or at least one in particular, and from the look on Devon's face, all was not well in Luckland.

CHAPTER EIGHT

"Devon, I must speak with you. Immediately."

Matilda loomed over our table, and I could tell by her expression something was wrong. She looked hurt—as if someone had just stabbed her in the back. That was the only way to describe it, but it couldn't have been Devon. He wouldn't hurt her for the world.

"Of course." He quickly stood, then gently steered her away, leaving Dani and me to ponder.

"Matilda must have found out about the concert and that we're going," I said, keeping my voice down. "That wouldn't be cause for alarm though. It's just a concert. Unless she thought we were going to try to meet Trey."

"How do you think she found out about it, if that's what's upsetting her?"

I shook my head. "I don't know. Perhaps she heard the others discussing it. That's a shame because it was meant to be a surprise."

Finn brought our drinks, and we went ahead and ordered our lasagna. I ordered for Devon. I wasn't sure when he'd be back inside, but I'd never hear the end of it if the food arrived and he didn't have any.

A few minutes later, Devon and Matilda came back, Matilda's expression now more serene. I looked up at him as they approached, hoping for a sign all was well and he'd reassured her about whatever her issue may have been. He winked at me. Either that was either my sign, or he was flirting. I'd take either.

He pulled up an extra chair for Matilda, and as she sat down between Dani and me, she took our hands and gave us each a squeeze.

"Sorry, girls. I didn't mean to disrupt things. Just a misunderstanding, but it's all fine." She raised her hand to signal Finn and end the discussion. Matilda was like that. When she decided to finish something, that was the end of it. She could be quite regal that way.

Finn came immediately, and she ordered herself some Harvest Pie. My heart sank. Going straight for dessert meant whatever had bothered her still bothered her.

When our food arrived, we chatted a little. Devon seemed completely unconcerned, but I worried about Matilda. We'd almost finished eating when she cleared her throat. "I have an announcement, and I don't want any of you to interfere."

"Interfere with your announcement?" That *was* a little odd.

"Don't be silly. I mean, don't interfere with what I'm going to do."

"And what is that, Aunt Tillie?" Dani asked.

I was pretty sure Matilda was about to tell us she was going to the concert, and we were not to try and stop her.

"I'm getting married," she stated. Quite emphatically.

My fork hit the plate with a resounding clang, though it didn't compare to the sound of Devon's glass shattering as it hit the floor. Dani sat wide-eyed, frozen, gripping her fork in mid-air.

I glanced at Devon, who looked as if he'd been hit with a sledgehammer. It was up to me to find out more. Taking a deep breath, I dove in.

"Married. I see." Proud I sounded quite normal, I smiled. "May I ask to whom?"

"Well, I don't know. I haven't met him yet."

That sure cleared that one up. A sudden gust of air signaled the arrival of the remaining posse members, my sister in tow. Great. All I wanted was a nice peaceful dinner with my favorite former G-man and my BFF. Instead, it appeared we'd be having some sort of impromptu meet-up at the café. At least I'd had my lasagna, so there was that.

I waited impatiently as the posse noisily dragged empty tables and chairs over to create a lovely not-so-private table. The remaining locals pretended to eat their dinner and mind their own business. I signaled Finn, who busily cleared the remains of Devon's shattering reaction. I needed another drink.

"And where is Dad this fine evening?" I asked my mom, knowing full well he would steer clear of this fiasco.

"He and Marty are over at the Manor with Tom," Babs whispered as she squeezed in between Devon and me.

"Why would Deputy Martin be over at the Manor with Tom and Dad?" I whispered back. "And why are we whispering?"

Babs just looked at me as if I should know. Sometimes I did, but at that moment, I could neither make heads nor tails of what was happening.

Finn made quick work of the broken glass and, thankfully, returned with two pitchers of sangria. He poured a drink for everyone, and the moment he was gone, Prudence leaned toward Devon.

"I assume Matilda told you her news, and you've talked her out of it, right?"

"She told us, but no, I haven't talked her out of anything. I need more information."

"Well, what more do you need to know?" asked my mom. "It's a ridiculous idea."

"Yes, Mom, we agree, though it would be helpful to have a bit more information, as Devon says," I said.

"Yes, Mother, maybe you can fill in the blanks for us as to what Matilda is thinking?" asked Babs, looking over at her, pleading.

"Maybe *Matilda* can explain it," said Matilda, referencing herself in the third person for emphasis.

"Please do." Devon took a very, very long swig of my drink. It appeared he'd finished his. Then he looked directly at his mother. "Go on, Mom, explain," he said in his full-on cope-mode voice. Since his mother was hell-bent on getting married to god knew who, he was entitled to be a little austere.

Matilda scrutinized those around the table, apparently making sure we were all paying attention. With a captive audience, she cleared her throat.

"Devon is all grown up. I'm alone."

"But you have all of us," my mom replied gently.

"Kate, you have Colin. Hope has Marcy. Prudence has Martin now. Me? I have nobody. I don't want to be alone. So, you see, I must find a husband immediately." She sighed dramatically.

We all glanced around the table in stunned silence, seemingly to seek affirmation we weren't the only ones confounded by Matilda's announcement. I looked at Devon. He knew her best and might be more inclined to understand what she was getting at. He wasn't. He looked absolutely lost.

"But I've come home now, so you still have me," he said, smiling softly.

My mom reached for Matilda's hand and held it while

trying her "soothing" tone. "Tillie, we all get lonely. That's what book clubs are for."

"And karaoke night," said Prudence.

I waited a beat, knowing Hope would be next.

"When those fail, there's always Barney," Hope declared with a soft laugh.

Barney? I quickly glanced at Devon. I'd clearly missed something. He obviously had as well.

I frowned. "Barney?"

A mortified moment of silence followed—until Prudence looked at me with raised eyebrows. *Oh.* Dani started snickering, Babs turned six shades of red, and if Devon's expression was anything to go by, he still had no idea who, or what, Barney was.

I leaned over and whispered in his ear. A bright streak of color flowed across Devon's cheeks. Too much information, apparently. Granted, like him, I hadn't wanted to know Matilda had a pet name for her sex toy, or even that she had a sex toy. Not that she shouldn't, I just never thought of her having those sorts of urges. Though I sincerely hoped when I was her age, I'd still be enjoying sex. With Devon.

"All well and good, but you aren't changing my mind. I visited Harriet Bumstead at the Luckland Mountain Care Center, and I do not want to be that woman," Matilda announced.

"What do you mean, *that woman*?" Devon asked. "Harriet is a perfectly nice lady."

"She's a perfectly lonely lady, is what she is. No family. No husband. No partner. Nothing. Nobody. She's all alone. She'll die that way. I won't have it," Matilda stated with finality.

"Well, you do have me, Mom," Devon said. "You won't die that way."

I shook my head in wonder. He really was that thick-headed sometimes.

"This is about Trey, isn't it, sweetie?" Hope asked, reaching over to clasp Matilda's hand.

Matilda looked off into the distance, a smile on her face.

"What are you thinking about, Tillie?" I remembered her telling us she had a cosmic connection with the Vegas lounge singer, but that was about it. Was she recalling that eventful night with Devon's father?

"Your mom looked so adorable wearing a Halloween bridal veil with a glittery tiara. The veil kept getting in the way every time she took a shot. She'd slam the shot glass down, and Prudence would wiggle her fingers and yell, 'One more round, barkeep.' Then she'd flash that infamous come-hither smile and shout, 'Make them doubles!' We'd all cheer. That was what we were there for. To celebrate with one another, you know? We'd all been together since forever."

Matilda took Devon's hand and squeezed it. More to comfort herself than Devon, I thought.

"Well, the bartender took it all in stride, of course. It was our second night in that place. Vegas is so very big and chaotic, and one has to find a special spot. Well, the one we found was very special."

Devon smiled. "Let me guess. Because of one particular vocalist? Tell me."

"Well, the room got dark, and Trey came on stage. 'Ready to go livin' on a prayer?' he whispered into the microphone as he fixed his gaze on mine. Then he reached out his hand. To me. Wanting *me* to come up and join him." She sighed, and her eyes sparkled.

"Hope jumped off her chair and yelled, 'Oh, you go, Matilda! Rock 'em out girl!' She's ordinarily so quiet and staid, but that night the old Hope had somehow turned into a new and bolder version of herself. Perhaps that last shot was one too many for her. Then I heard Kate yell something about me flashing. Or was it no flashing? Pru stood on her chair, wobbling and shushing everyone."

Matilda sighed again. "Well, he started to sing, and I joined in, and it was magic. Our voices were in perfect harmony. Suddenly, people started to crowd around to listen. It was so exciting. After his set, he joined us for some champagne. Then it was au revoir to my handsome crooner."

"Tillie, did you skip something?" I asked because clearly Devon wasn't conceived that night.

"What do you mean?"

"Well, if you said goodbye to your crooner, when exactly did you, um, well..." I didn't quite know how to phrase it.

Devon looked at me, horrified. If he'd ever thought of his conception, it seemed he'd done so clinically. It was all DNA to him.

"Oh, I see. I'd actually met Trey the night before. Pru and I wanted to stay out a little later, and after Kate and Hope went to our hotel, Pru and I stayed for another set. Then Pru left."

Devon leaned forward, waiting for more, but I tapped him on the knee and shook my head ever so slightly. Some memories should remain private. Even I knew that. Time to switch gears.

"Matilda, why don't you tell us your plan to get married, so we can all understand what you intend?" I asked.

With a smile, she launched into an explanation about an online service called "Second Chances" that specialized in finding soulmates for the over-fifty generation. Basically, she'd fill out a profile, then start chatting online with prospective "life mates" until she found someone she'd like to meet in person. Seemed pretty much standard fare for an online dating site. She clearly wasn't aware of what the ladies planned for her birth-day. So, all we had to do was stall.

"Tillie, you know I work with a ton of wedding planners, and they know all the best dating sites. Let me contact a few and see who they recommend. Will you at least let me do that for you?" That would buy us enough time for her to go to Denver and see Trey again, then drop the whole dating idea. However, Matilda *had* seen Trey at least once since she'd had Devon. What happened there? Devon and I needed to find out before the concert.

"All right, Pippa. You find me three sites to choose from that you all *approve* of, and I will choose one of those. Are we all in agreement that I may proceed then?" Matilda asked.

There were nods and murmurs around the table. At least everyone seemed to be on board. I wasn't positive about Devon, but I hoped he trusted my judgment on this one.

"Good. Now that's settled, let's discuss the plan for next week," Matilda said. "My birthday surprise. What do you all have planned?"

CHAPTER NINE

Devon, Dani, and I left the café and returned to the house. I mulled over what ridiculous story the ladies might concoct to appease Matilda. With less than a week to go before the concert, it couldn't be that hard to keep her in the dark, but Matilda, ever the party planner and famous for her soirées, would not sit idly by and allow her sixtieth birthday to pass without fanfare.

The moment we arrived home, Dani disappeared upstairs with the excuse that she needed to work on an instructional manual for her diving course—which could mean she had a good trashy novel stashed away. Devon liked to pick up my stray steamy books and read passages aloud. Totally not funny. Somehow, all the heat got lost in translation.

"We've got quite a bit to unpack, don't we, Pip," Devon said as we settled on the sofa, and he rested his chin on my head.

I sighed. "Yeah, it's been quite the day. So, where do we start? I'm assuming you don't want to discuss Barney." I laughed out loud, and his chest shook as he laughed as well.

"Quite right. We can discuss that later. First, when my mom pulled me outside the café, she was upset because she'd expected the ladies to be all abuzz about her birthday, and nobody had said a word about it. She assumed there would be a surprise party, and she'd have heard about it through the grapevine."

"What does she not understand about the word 'surprise'?"

Devon grinned. "Anyway, I reassured her that plans were in the works and to be patient."

"That's it?"

"Until she dropped her bombshell and announced her crazy-ass plan to get married."

"Don't worry about that. We'll stall her until the posse get her to the concert. Then we'll play it by ear."

"Okay. So, about your visions. I've thought about this, and I know what you saw."

I sat up abruptly, banging my head on his chin in the process. "Ow." I put my hand on my head, looked up, and gave him my best apologetic smile. Then I leaned up to kiss him. Worked every time. In fact, I sometimes thought he used my lack of grace to his advantage. Not that I minded. "What were they?"

"Miners," he stated. "Gold miners."

I frowned. "Both of them?"

"Well, certainly the second one. I'm not sure about the one near the barn, but it kind of makes sense that two men from that era suddenly show themselves to you."

"Does it? How?"

"Well, we've had a lot of talk about Luckland's gold and spirits recently. Perhaps the ghosts are—"

"Trying to tell us there's gold in them thar hills..."

Devon laughed. "Could be."

"Actually, I think you're right. Somehow, somebody is trying to tell me where to find the gold."

"If it exists. And if it does, that means it's not in our yard."

I couldn't quite tell, but I thought I detected a note of facetiousness there, though I did agree with him that the entire episode of digging around our house was quite bothersome.

"What's next on the discussion list?" he asked.

"I would like to know what you and Simon have been up to these past few days. You're no longer with the FBI, and I'm pretty sure they wouldn't call you back in on a case."

"Inter-agency stuff, Pip. Happens all the time."

No, it didn't. He was the one and only officer in Luckland's police department, and there hadn't been any crimes. He was clearly hiding something, but I kept my suspicions to myself and moved on.

"Okay, I'd like to talk about Morgan."

That seemed to surprise Devon because he frowned. "Morgan? Why?"

"Well, I don't know if you noticed, but at lunch, she looked at her phone and seemed to freeze for a moment. I think she got a text that spooked her." I didn't like Morgan, but I didn't want to see her upset, and she definitely appeared upset.

"Do you think it's something I should worry about as a cop?"

"I don't know, but something didn't seem right. Maybe it's guy trouble."

"I didn't know she was dating anyone."

For a police officer, Devon sometimes lacked observation skills.

"Hunter Jackson," I said. "I saw them in a very hot lip lock at the gazebo the other night."

"Who is Hunter Jackson?"

"One of the crew Tom hired for the reno on the house."

"You know him by name?"

"Single guys who come to Luckland to work on a temporary

gig are bound to hit on the local women..." I let that dangle there and grinned.

"You said no, yeah?" Devon almost looked worried.

"I said, no, yeah." I smiled and leaned up just as he leaned down for a kiss.

"Then maybe you should keep an eye on her. Make sure this Hunter Jackson isn't trying to take advantage, especially if he's only here temporarily," Devon said. "Meanwhile, I'll do a little research of my own. I wonder if maybe there are some recorded historical references to apparitions of miners over the years."

Normally, I got the research, and he got to spy on people. The role reversal was perfect, though, mainly because I didn't want him anywhere near Morgan. Perhaps he knew that. Whatever his motivation, I was fine with his plan.

The following morning, I headed to the café on my way to the shop while Dani stayed back to work on her instructional manual. Morgan wasn't always on shift early in the day, but I spotted her car turning into the alley behind the café and took a chance. I waited a few minutes and let her settle in before I headed inside. She greeted me pretty warmly, which wasn't unusual since I was alone. She was quite friendly and personable when not in the presence of Devon. Or any other even remotely attractive man, for that matter. I sat at the counter and ordered a coffee and cinnamon roll. I'd already made a mental list of questions to ask, keeping them mostly impersonal. Chitchat. I hoped she wouldn't question my friendliness, but I didn't have to worry—it appeared she was all set for some girl talk.

Setting my cinnamon roll in front of me, she flipped a waiting mug right side up and began talking as she poured.

"So, guess who I saw out at the Starlight Bistro on Route 19 last night?"

"I'll bite. Who'd you see?" I grinned. This could be good.

"Prudence. With that deputy. They really are sweet." Morgan sighed. She actually sighed.

"Yeah, they make a good pair. So, you were out at the bistro last night. Hot date?"

"Very hot. Sizzling, if you must know."

"Let me guess, that Hunter guy. I noticed you were getting cozy over at the gazebo."

Morgan giggled. "Seriously, he's amazing. He's actually been around the world and was almost in the fifty most beautiful people edition of Adventure Island Magazine. Plus, he's got big hands." She smiled and winked. Dear lord, save me.

I was pretty sure there was no such magazine, and I wondered how much bullshit he was feeding her.

"Did you know he's a race car driver?"

That caught my attention. If I hadn't known about Dad's cars in the barn, Morgan's statement would have gone right over my head, but I sat up, suddenly interested.

"Wow, what kind?" I asked as innocently as possible.

"Oh, those little low ones. They look like hot dogs, you know."

In other words, she didn't know what they were called. Or she did and didn't want me to know.

Morgan grinned. "Not just that, but Hunter is quite brilliant. He graduated with honors from the School of Mines."

Mines? With my spidey senses on high alert, I leaned closer. "Sounds as if he's quite the catch." The only thing I'd known about Hunter was that he'd moved into town a few months earlier, but if he was a School of Mines graduate, why was he working on a construction crew? In Luckland?

"Oh, he is."

Since she couldn't have Devon, it seemed she was trying to one-up me in the hot guy department. Hunter was an attractive guy, but I wasn't into the surfer dude thing. I preferred the intellectual type. Like Devon.

"So, he didn't text you yesterday to break a date or anything? Just that I noticed you seemed upset when you looked at your phone at lunch."

Morgan frowned. "No, of course not. He was just— Well, it's fine."

I nodded. "Good. Don't let him take advantage of you," I said. Then, not wanting to show any more interest in Hunter, I hurriedly finished my breakfast and headed to the shop to do some serious investigating on my laptop.

CHAPTER TEN

WATCHING DEVON IN THE KITCHEN, I STUDIED HIS PROFILE. HE REALLY did have some exquisite genes. Strong chiseled jawline, slightly tousled golden-brown hair, and some serious muscle tone. Add in the intelligence factor, and he was pretty much my idea of a perfect man, especially when he cleaned up after a dinner he cooked. The man was a keeper.

He caught me staring and entered the den, where I had made myself comfortable on the sofa. Dani had once again retreated upstairs.

"Well, Pip, what have you got?" He picked up my legs and sat before he lightly brushed the hair off my face, distracting me.

After a moment, I remembered what I was supposed to tell him. "Well, I spoke to Morgan, and she's definitely dating Hunter Jackson."

"And? Clearly, there's more?"

"Yes, yes, there is, but you'll have to tell me something as well. What have you learned?"

"Ah. I see how this is played. Okay then. Did you know that

in 1849 a navigational star map went missing from the home of Archibald Stelton in Beacon Hill, Boston?"

"Oh, that's the highbrow neighborhood, right?" That was where the money was back then. At least according to my historical romance novels.

"Yes, precisely so, which opens the possibility that it might just have been the legendary map leading to the Luckland gold. My theory? It was stolen in 1849, then purchased by our esteemed town fathers in a local tavern sometime after that."

"Well, considering they bought the map for only twenty-five cents, it's not too much of a stretch to think it had been stolen."

"Agreed, but what is even more interesting is how I found out who the map might have belonged to. I was researching regional stories and tales of ghostly sightings. I came upon a story about a man who disappeared in the mountains of Colorado around 1855. The locals report seeing his ghost meandering the area."

"And?"

"The ghost was reported to be a male dwarf. A man whose name is—"

"Archibald Stelton! So, Archie came to Colorado, *without* his precious map because someone had stolen it, to find the gold and ended up dead and haunting the area. How did he die? Did he discover gold? What about his family?"

Devon shrugged. "There is no further information on him. So, if he did find any gold, it was never disclosed."

"Maybe he found it but didn't have time to tell anyone before he died."

"Maybe."

"Or maybe he didn't find it because our ancestors had already dug it up and hid it."

"Both those possibilities could be true, and we may never know, but at least we know whose ghost you saw."

"One of them. We still have no idea about the one near the barn or the child you saw on the road."

"Well, no, but I can keep looking if you want."

I shook my head. Knowing the names of the ghosts wouldn't really make a difference. "So, you believe in ghosts now?"

Devon smiled. "I don't think we can discount the possibility, but it's not something I really want to go around telling people."

"No, I guess not. Imagine what our mothers would say. They'd be sitting us around in a circle ready to hold a séance." I shuddered in emphasis, and Devon laughed.

"So, my news. Hunter Jackson has a Master's in Metallurgical Engineering, a PhD in Mining Engineering, and studied Astronomy as an undergraduate." I waited for Devon to react, which he did by jumping up and dumping me on the floor in the process. Then he began pacing back and forth, analyzing information out loud.

"A mining engineer with a background in astronomy moves to Luckland to work as a construction crewman. An odd career choice. I don't think it's a stretch to imagine he knows about the founders' map." He abruptly stopped when he realized I was in the middle of peeling myself off the floor. He reached down and pulled me up. With a quick kiss, he deposited me back on the sofa. "What else do you have?"

"Not much more, I'm afraid. Except Morgan is pretty smitten with this guy. I have a feeling she'd do anything he asked of her. Oh, and he's a race car driver."

Devon stared at me. "Is that significant?"

"I don't know. I mean, I wouldn't have even mentioned it,

except I now know about the cars in the barn—that may or may not be protected by a ghost."

"Right now, I wouldn't discount anything, but let's focus on the budding romantics and what they're up to."

"I thought *we* were the budding romantics!" I eyed him and raised my brows.

"Quite right, duly noted." Devon pulled me off the couch and wrapped his arms around me. "How about we go up and have that discussion now," he said quite mischievously.

"Discussion?"

"Yes, about Barney." He winked.

"Oh, Rosa, take a look at this!"

Dani and I froze at the sound of my mother's voice in the dressing room next door. If our moms were there, that could only mean the others weren't far behind. In all fairness, they probably had the same idea we had—to come to the mall and search for the perfect outfit for the upcoming concert, which was a momentous event with Trey and Matilda hopefully reuniting and a possible backstage visit with a photo op with The Raskins.

"Oh, Tillie, try this!" Dani's mom exclaimed from somewhere in the dressing room area.

Dani held one finger in front of her mouth and nodded, indicating we should slip out quietly. However, we'd been trying on lingerie—and not the kind we wanted our mothers to see. It then occurred to me that perhaps they were doing the same. Not a concept I wanted floating around in my head.

We quickly changed back into our clothes. Dani opened the curtain enough to peek out and shook her head. We were not going to escape undetected, so she simply opened the curtain all the way and stepped out in full view.

"What are you doing here, girls?" My mother appeared shocked by our presence, as were Prudence and Hope standing beside her.

"We could ask the same of you." I gave her a bit of a squinty-eyed look—the one that said I knew what she was up to, which was what we were up to. However, they didn't know we were also attending the show.

Dani quickly stepped forward and gave Rosa a hug. "Mom, it's lovely to see you."

Matilda emerged from the dressing room wearing what had to be the hottest little red dress I had ever seen. She was tall, lithe, and elegant and could easily carry the dress off, regardless of her age.

I sighed, wishing I could be that drop-dead gorgeous. "You look beautiful, Tillie."

"She does, doesn't she," Prudence said, beaming at us. "So, what are you shopping for? Hot dates?" Nothing fired up Prudence like our love lives.

"Good guess," replied Dani with a grin. "Devon is bringing his buddy Simon out with us."

I was astonished she'd admit to being interested in anyone, considering doing so was an invitation for the ladies to meddle. The ladies already constantly interfered as Devon and I navigated our way through a new relationship.

"Simon was at our last shindig. I remember him well." Tillie smiled. "He certainly is a looker!"

I decided right then to add cougar to the list of labels we had for these women. There was no taming them.

"You certainly can't wear the same outfits as last time," Rosa commented.

"Absolutely not," said my mom. "So, where are you going? Dinner? A movie? A show?"

Uh-oh. We certainly couldn't tell them we were going to the concert, so we needed some fast thinking. Dani came to the rescue, which she always did when we didn't want the women to know what we were up to.

"We don't know for sure, but we were informed it would be nothing fancy, just a casual evening."

Perfect.

"No such thing as casual when you're on a date," said Hope. "Perhaps some new accessories will help?"

I hoped she meant accessories, as in jewelry or scarves. Nope. The look on her face meant something else entirely.

"We've got to go, Dani." I grabbed her elbow, then yanked her alongside me as I headed toward the exit. "We'll catch up with you later," I called out to the ladies as Dani and I hurried out of the shop. It was a close call. Had we stayed any longer, the posse would have raided the women's lingerie department, and we'd end up trying on the kind of lingerie models wore on the covers of those trashy novels I liked to read when Devon was otherwise occupied.

We decided to head back home, then sneak back to the mall later and get the things we'd left behind in the dressing room.

Just as we'd settled on my sofa to relax, our phones lit up like the Fourth of July with texts.

Matilda: My house. Pronto.

Mom: Tillie's. Now.

Prudence: Hurry to Tillie's.

Hope: Emergency at Tillie's.

CHAPTER ELEVEN

"ONE AT A TIME, LADIES, PLEASE." DEVON RAISED HIS VOICE ABOVE THE chatter. The posse had gathered in Matilda's kitchen. Dani, Devon, and I had raced over, thinking there had been an emergency. For the ladies, there was. It seemed something had gone missing. Something was always going missing in Matilda's house though. She was that lady who would lose the car keys in her hand and the glasses atop her head. She'd lose that too if it weren't attached.

"Look at the wall, Devon. Just look!" Matilda was in full-on hysterics.

We all looked at the wall. Then back at one another.

"What am I looking at, Mom?" he asked.

"What do you see?"

"Nothing. There is nothing there." He tipped his head in confusion.

"Precisely, dear boy! It's gone!"

I couldn't remember what had been there. Something in a frame—if the faded imprint on the paint was any indication. I peered at Devon to see if he remembered. He looked thoughtful as if running a search function in his brain.

"Wasn't it just a silly painting of mine from that summer art program you forced us into?" From his expression, it looked as if he wondered who would care about such a thing.

"It wasn't silly," replied Matilda.

"I know you're sentimental, but it's not as if it was a Rembrandt." Devon smiled, which I believed was to calm her down.

Matilda glanced at her comrades. They all exchanged one of their very suspicious looks. Then she turned back to Devon. "It was the map. The map was hidden behind the painting." Matilda flopped across the sofa as if totally wiped out from the exchange.

"Which map is that, Tillie?" I asked in as calm a voice as possible. I knew. I absolutely knew it was the navigational map. Impossible as it should be, what other map would she be talking about?

"The map that led our pioneering ancestors here to Luckland."

"The one that's supposed to be in a display case in the town hall?" Devon asked.

I would have expected him to be furious, but he appeared strangely calm. Too calm.

"It was never in a display case. That was something one of our ancestors made up to fool anyone who came looking for the gold. The original could never be left where everyone could see it."

Devon shook his head. "So, you kept the original here? Behind my painting?"

I worried Devon was going to lose his cool. A valuable artifact the town was famous for wasn't even authentic or where it was supposed to be.

"Well, it wasn't always here. We took it in turns to keep it safe."

"You took turns?" Devon sighed. "What about a copy? Did you have a copy of it?"

"I had the copy," my mother said. "It was in Uncle Ernie's box."

Oh god, the shoeboxes again. My stomach dropped. That was why the ladies had gone ballistic and called Devon, who came home to help find them. The fact they were still missing wasn't good, but at least I was getting an idea of how some of the mysteries Devon and I had yet to solve were linked.

I sat beside Matilda and took her hand. "When did you realize it was missing, Tillie?" I asked as a way to keep her calm and focused.

"When I got home from the mall. I'm certain it was there when I left today."

"Are you sure?" Devon asked. "Is it possible it's been missing for a while, and you didn't notice?"

"Quite sure, my boy. As you are aware, before I leave the house, I always, always tap the picture. It's good luck."

"Honestly, I just thought you were a bit neurotic about straightening it out," Devon remarked. "I didn't realize it was a superstitious thing."

Matilda launched herself off the couch and sauntered over to huddle with the other women. That was never good. They began whispering, which was also never a good thing.

"Ladies. Care to share?" Devon used his polite tone, which didn't mean he'd tempered his frustration.

Hope turned to us and smiled her very stoic librarian smile that indicated whatever she was going to say would be the last word. I braced myself.

"Probably best if you all went on your way. We'll take care of this," she said with a great deal of finality. I looked at Devon to see if he'd acquiesce or push back. Push back. It was all over his face. The set jaw. The clenched teeth. The laser-focused eyes.

"No can do, Hope. Someone stole that map, and I'm going to have to dust for fingerprints and look around. Then we'll go. On second thought, why don't you all reconvene somewhere while I see to this."

"Very well," said my mother, who would be perfectly happy to head out if it meant she could avoid answering more questions. She took Rosa by the arm and marched out with Matilda, Prudence, Hope, and Marcy right behind. That left Dani and me to figure out whether we should stay or go.

"I think you two can head on back to the house. I got this." Devon tipped his head and held out an arm to direct us toward the front door. If Devon wasn't my significant other, I'd take into consideration he was a cop and there was no need to hang around while he did his thing. Something in his voice, however, sent a tingling sensation up my spine. I looked at Dani to see if she also noticed something suspicious in his tone. She nodded and folded her arms across her chest. I did the same. We turned to face him, bracing for the argument ahead.

"Spill it, secret agent man. Why do you want us all gone?" I narrowed my eyes as I spoke.

"I'm kind of curious too, Dev. Don't think we didn't notice you texting somebody a second ago," Dani said.

I tried not to show any reaction to what Dani had just said because I had no idea Devon had texted anyone. Dani must have been paying attention. Generally, I was observant, but the posse had me distracted.

Devon pursed his lips as he contemplated his response. "I was just confirming things with Simon."

What he said was plausible, but then again, he didn't say what he was confirming.

"Confirming what, exactly?" I asked.

"You know, our plans," he said vaguely while he examined the wall.

"Plans for?" Dani asked.

We knew Devon was implying it was about our plans to see The Raskins, but he didn't actually say it, and with Devon, who was very clever and careful with his words, what he didn't say was as important as what he did say. Every word mattered.

We waited patiently for his answer. Suddenly, his phone buzzed. Devon looked down at the screen, wrinkled his brow, muttered an apology, and ran out the front door.

Not being the sort of women who liked to be left behind, we raced after him.

CHAPTER TWELVE

Gone. He had simply disappeared. His latest rental car was in the driveway, but Devon had vanished. Because Dani and I had hesitated a second too long before chasing after him, that must have given him enough lead time to hop into someone else's car.

"Simon," Dani said. Then she sighed.

"What are they up to?"

We looked at each other in a silent conversation where we agreed we needed a glass of wine to help get some answers. When we got back to my place, I went straight to the fridge, grabbed a bottle of rosé, and headed for the couch while Dani grabbed some snacks. Whatever the boys were doing, they'd purposely left us girls out of it, which Devon would surely pay for later.

99 joined us on the sofa, snuggling cozily between us, covering her eyes with her paws as she napped.

After a fortifying sip of wine, I turned to Dani. "Did you notice Devon left without getting those fingerprints? He didn't even take a picture of the wall. He knows where that map went."

"You think he took it? But why would he?"

I had an idea. "It wouldn't surprise me if he took it for safe-keeping. There are too many people who believe the gold exists, and if they believe it exists, they'll be after the map."

"But wouldn't they, whoever *they* are, take pictures of the one at the town hall?"

"I'm sure they already have, and if they've figured it's not authentic, then they'd come looking for the original, and if they had any knowledge of who the four founders' descendants were, then their targets would be the women." The ominous phone calls the ladies all received, claiming someone knew their secrets, made me wonder if those secrets included the map. Maybe whoever had the shoeboxes already had the copy of the map. Devon hadn't known Mom had a copy in one of the shoeboxes though. I guess that was a bigger incentive to find them.

"So, Devon took the map so no one else could," Dani said.

"It's certainly conceivable."

"Are you going to ask him if he took it?"

It was a good question, and I internally debated the best course of action. "Let's see if he'll voluntarily come clean about his nefarious actions without us prompting him, though I have a feeling he won't say a thing. He's becoming more secretive than the ladies."

A few hours later, after Dani and I had consumed another bottle of rosé, Devon and Simon strolled in, all casual-like. Devon grinned at me, but I refused to smile back willingly.

"Hungry?" He held up a bag before I could ask him why he'd disappeared on us.

I squinted at him as my stomach rumbled. "What's in there?"

"A surprise." That earned him a glare, and he laughed. "If

you sit yourselves down at the table, it's possible we'll share it with you."

I held up one hand and allowed him to pull me up. I would never say no to food.

My chic but small dining table felt more like a snack tray with all four of us. Devon was a big guy, but Simon seemed to fill every bit of space. He was also quite easy on the eyes as he looked a little like Dwayne "The Rock" Johnson. Though seating at the table might have been cramped, the food most definitely made up for it. Bison short rib sliders from the Blue Sky Café were a particular favorite of mine. I tried to be graceful about eating, but barbecue sauce was messy. Dani always ate as if having tea with the queen. Everything Dani did, she did with grace. Even when diving. She could strap a thirty-five-pound scuba tank on her back and dive like a swan.

Simon seemed preoccupied as he leaned back, admiring Dani with more than a little interest. He was so focused on her he wasn't eating. That, or he just wasn't hungry. Dani must have also noticed.

"Can I help you with something?" She smiled as she said it, so it didn't come off too snarky.

"I'm good. Just enjoying the view." He grinned, which elicited an elbow from Devon and a shake of his head.

Dani's response was to cross her arms and stare right back.

If nothing else, the entire exchange was quite entertaining. Dani could handle herself and wasn't easily rattled, but I sensed she found Simon a little unnerving. She wouldn't let him know that, but I knew.

"So, Simon, what were you two boys up to this afternoon?" I asked.

He turned his head only slightly away from Dani to look at me, then shook his head and laughed. "Nothing too fascinating, just a few errands."

"I see." I looked at Devon to gauge his guilt level. High. Definitely high.

"Devon, did you, by any chance, locate the missing map?" I was setting him up, and he knew it.

"No, no luck."

Dani sat forward in her chair. "Interesting. You should have hit up that antiquities shop near Market Street in Denver. I hear the owner is some sort of map aficionado. Everything from underwater topography to star navigation. He even has some of the new bathymetric maps." Dani sat back and gloated, waiting for their reaction.

The guys glanced at each other, then quickly focused their attention back on us. I always knew when Devon suspected I was up to something. He would stare so hard it was as if he tried to see into my brain. It appeared Simon had that same habit—only he fixed his gaze on Dani.

"Explain." Simon raised his eyebrows, another of those looks I knew so well from Devon.

"A Well-Worn Odyssey," said Dani. "Anyone who dives knows of it."

Considering Dani and I had concluded Devon had taken the map, I wasn't sure why she was talking about map stores. I was just about to ask her when Devon kicked me under the table. Not hard. Just a warning tap. I glanced over, and he shook his head slightly. I frowned, unsure what he was up to, but then I decided to give him the benefit of the doubt. He sure was amassing a whole lot of IOUs though.

"I see," replied Simon. "Since I do dive but am not familiar with this place, perhaps you'll take me there. Say tomorrow?"

By Dani's lack of reaction, Simon had taken her completely off guard.

"It's settled then. I'll pick you up at nine." Simon smiled, then stood and began clearing the table.

Dani looked at me. Her expression half excitement and half terror. Simon had roped her into taking him map hunting, but in this case, she was the one who'd provided the rope. Unless we accused Devon of taking the map, which we'd agreed not to, she couldn't call Simon's bluff.

"We'll have to be back by early afternoon as the show's tomorrow night," Dani said, which might have been her way of looking for a reprieve.

"No worries. If we run late, we'll meet up at the theater," Simon replied.

I laughed so hard I snorted. Literally. He called it a theater. The Organ Grinder was a well-known nostalgic rock venue. The kind with a mosh pit and sticky walls. Some of the best bands ever had played there.

Simon looked at me curiously but didn't ask. Devon also gave me a curious look, which was when I realized he'd never been there either.

Table cleared and discussion apparently over, Devon escorted Simon to the door while Dani and I resumed our comfortable positions on the couch. October meant non-stop reruns of our favorite Halloween movie, *Hocus Pocus*. We knew every line and recited them in turn. Fleetingly, I wondered if Devon would hang around and make it awkward or head upstairs and let Dani and me have our fun. The younger version of Devon would have hung around and teased us, so I was hoping he'd outgrown that.

He dashed my hopes when he returned. He saw we were cozying up to watch a movie and said he'd make some popcorn.

He returned a few minutes later, placed one bowl on the coffee table for us, and sat in the recliner with his own bowl in hand. He didn't ask what we were watching but smirked when it started.

"Only one rule here, Sir Interloper," I said to him. "No comments, and no making fun."

"And no throwing popcorn," said Dani for good measure. Devon was that kid a few rows back at the movies who liked to throw popcorn at us, especially when we had dates. He still did. I couldn't take him anywhere.

"Where is Simon staying? The Inn?" I noticed he was always only minutes away. He'd made a habit of staying with us, but with Dani occupying the guest room, I assumed he found other accommodation.

"Not sure," Devon mumbled through a mouthful of popcorn. He might have mumbled something else, but I was pretty sure he didn't want me to clearly understand whatever it was.

He didn't last more than a half hour. It seemed he just wasn't a Hocus Pocus fan. He left us alone so Dani and I could totally relax and enjoy the movie, which we did, quite enthusiastically. I was sure Devon wondered what all the shouting was when we got to the good stuff. We stayed up when it was over to gab for a while, then headed to bed as Dani had to get up and get primed in the morning. When she was out on a dive, she was up at the crack of dawn, so she changed things up when she could and slept in. Simon had nixed that, though I had a feeling she didn't mind all that much.

The next morning, Simon and Dani headed up to Denver. We'd planned to meet for dinner before the show, then get to the *theater* before the posse. We needed to prepare ourselves for any eventuality.

CHAPTER THIRTEEN

Devon and I met Simon and Dani, who looked awfully chummy, at a gastropub around the corner from The Organ Grinder.

"So, what did you find out at the map store?" I asked as soon as we'd settled at a table. Devon still hadn't said anything about him taking the map, and a tiny, niggly part of me wondered if he had, but who else could it have been?

"It was closed." Simon took out his phone and showed us the sign on the shop's front door.

I thought taking a picture of a sign was a bit odd, but Devon peered closely and nodded at Simon. Some sort of secret language between them.

"Why the picture?" I was curious about what those boys were thinking.

Dani looked at me and shook her head as if to say, *don't even go there*. Hmmm.

"It's always best to keep an accurate record," Devon replied. "Could be something we're missing."

"If the shop was closed, what did you two do all afternoon?" I looked at Dani with suspicion. She shrugged and smiled, then said The Denver Zoo had some interesting exhibits. I didn't buy a word of it.

Frustrated I wasn't getting any answers, though I probably hadn't asked the right questions, I ordered what I could only describe as a colossal margarita, and though talk flowed during dinner, I couldn't help but feel Devon and Simon were still keeping secrets. As soon as I got Devon alone, I was going to ask him about the map.

Dinner over, we headed to the club, and as soon as we arrived, Simon and Devon stopped short, staring at the window as if they'd seen a ghost. I had to nudge Devon out of the way because he was so tall, I couldn't peer over his shoulder.

At first, I had no idea what was wrong. Stuck to the window was a poster with a pretty hot photo of The Raskins. Just below the image, it declared, "With Special Guest Trey Marks." Or it used to. Someone had taken a Sharpie to the poster, and it seemed there'd be no special guest.

"Could be someone just vandalizing the poster," I said softly.

"Nope. I feel it, Pip. Something is not right in the Mile High City tonight." Devon's voice was a little sarcastic right about then. Not typical for Devon. He was a straight shooter most of the time. Sarcasm wasn't usually his thing. Then again, he'd been ready to see his dad for the first time, and his dreams had just been smashed to smithereens, so he was entitled to a little off-centered remark or two.

"Probably right, Kemosabe. Shall we get in line?" I asked, knowing he may want to bail. He looked disappointed.

"What's the point? He's not here," he said.

"The point is that Dani and I have no intention of leaving without a few photos with The Raskins. They always offer photo opportunities."

He narrowed his eyes. Spark of jealousy, perhaps? That always gave me warm fuzzies.

"Dani, please explain to these two we aren't leaving without our selfies."

"We're not leaving without our selfies," she said with a laugh.

"Besides, don't you want to be here when the posse arrives?" I asked.

"No need to, as they'll probably all just turn around and go home." Devon was probably right. Once the women got hold of an idea, they rarely deviated, and their idea was to join Matilda and Trey. If Trey wasn't here, there wouldn't be any reason for them to be here either.

Right on cue, they marched down the sidewalk. No, not marched. Sashayed. Swinging their hips, arm in arm, dressed to the nines with a blindfolded Matilda treading along carefully in the middle. I could sense the impending doom of disappointment about to overtake them. I cringed and braced myself.

They all stopped short. Matilda began to nervously turn her head every which way. They were only a few feet from us. My mother stepped forward and glared at me, then took a few more steps to close the distance.

"What are you doing here?" she whispered.

I took a deep breath, primarily to counter the margarita effect. "Same thing you are, Mom, but it's not happening," I whispered back as I pointed to the sign.

"Oh, for the love of Saint Maybelline," she said, no longer whispering. "If that's not a pile of monkey dung in a pigsty, I don't know what is."

That was the first time I'd ever heard my mother swear so colorfully. I burst into laughter. The situation itself wasn't funny but being tipsy and hearing such fun things from Mom, I couldn't help it. Dani grinned. Devon and Simon appeared stunned.

My mom spun around, waved at the others to indicate they could remove the blindfold, then headed back to them. They huddled and whispered, then turned and began walking away.

"You better go see what they're up to, Pip. I don't like this." Devon sounded worried. I was too. I grabbed Dani and hurried after them.

Naturally, we had every intention of returning. We were just going to see what the women were doing, thinking, or planning. I hadn't considered the possibility Dani and I would end up following the ladies into their RV. Nor did I plan on getting cozy on the couch while we relaxed and caught our breath. I certainly didn't intend to remain on the RV as it pulled out of the parking lot, headed for destinations unknown.

However, that was what we did.

CHAPTER FOURTEEN

THE LAST TIME I ENDED UP ON A ROAD TRIP WITH MOM AND THE besties, Devon was along for the ride, and I'd practically proclaimed my undying love on the intercom system—which was why this motor beast didn't hold fond memories for me. From the horror on Dani's face as the monster kicked into gear, she wasn't too thrilled either. However, her expression also showed shock and awe. This particular RV was no ordinary leisure travel craft. It was a fully loaded, half-a-million-dollar luxury mobile. I'd told her about it, of course, but clearly, she hadn't quite believed me.

"Mama." Dani looked at Rosa, who sat in the leather banquette with Matilda, Hope, and Marcy. Prudence drove, and my mom rode shotgun. "I think you have some 'splainin' to do!" Inside joke in her family. Something to do with the legendary Ricky Ricardo.

"All in good time, baby girl!" Rosa said, shushing her. "Right now, we've got to figure out a game plan."

I sat forward in my chair. "Maybe we can help *if* we know what the game is?"

Hope swiveled around to face us. "Girls, clearly we were

planning a surprise for Matilda, which fell through." She glanced at Matilda, smiled softly, then turned back to us. "Naturally, we've got a plan B. Not our first rodeo, dear."

"I'm guessing we're headed there now. Which is where?" I honestly didn't know why I'd asked because I knew I wouldn't get a straight answer.

"I suppose you'll just have to wait and see." With that, she turned back around with a great deal of finality, which meant we were in for a road trip. I texted the good news to Devon. Dani looked peeved. I had an idea she'd been enjoying her time with Simon, and by now, the nice little buzz from the margarita had worn off.

"I don't suppose there are cocktails on board?" I asked in a cheerful tone.

Marcy jumped up and smiled. "Who's up for a daiquiri?" She headed to the full-size fridge, which they'd no doubt fully stocked, and began pulling out all kinds of fresh fruit. Hope followed to retrieve the blender, and the two began whirring away.

When my phone buzzed, I knew it was Devon.

Devon: Where r u headed?

Me: No clue, but it's plan B.

Devon: Let me know when you arrive.

Me: Aye, Aye, Captain.

Considering my mom rode shotgun, I figured she oversaw directions and final destinations. Maybe I could find out from her.

"Mom, I assume we'll be stopping for a break at some point, correct?"

"Probably."

"Well, why don't you tell me where we're going, and Dani and I can find a good spot to stop?" I thought that was a great idea, and it would give us a heads-up.

Mom shook her head. "I don't want to ruin the surprise."

"We don't want to be surprised."

At my mom's infuriatingly bland expression, I sighed. "Can you at least tell us what route we're taking?"

"Fine, we'll be headed through Albuquerque," my mom said. That was the last clear statement we got before Marcy turned on the blender for daiquiris and Matilda turned on the dreaded karaoke. It wasn't enough to just turn on some driving tunes with these women. Oh no. It was always showtime.

I was surprised Rosa started the party. Dani's mom usually sat back and let things simply happen around her. Not that night. Apparently, she was in a mood and did her best Gloria Estefan impression. She swung her hips and even shook her boobs a few times.

Dani grinned and drank up as she watched her mother cut loose. I prayed my mother wasn't up next. Thankfully, I my phone went off and spared me, though I groaned at the ring-tone, which Devon liked to toy with. Instead of a simple jingle, Rod Stewart's *Do you think I'm sexy* blared from my phone. My mother, along with the other female guardians of the clan, suddenly became quiet as mice and stared at me. Smirking.

Kill me now.

I hurried to the cabin in the back of the RV and shut the door before I sat on one of the bunks and answered the call.

"What is it?" I whispered. The women were probably all standing out there, holding glasses against the door to listen in. "And please, for the love of god, stop messing with my phone."

I shook my head as he laughed. I could picture him grinning from ear to ear and probably elbowing Simon in the process.

"So, where are you headed, and what's plan B?" he finally managed to ask.

"Don't know, but I assume it's got something to do with

Trey. I promise to call you as soon as I find out or when we get there."

"Okay, or text it to me."

"I might. Then again..." It was my turn to laugh before I ended the call. I missed him. Funny how at the oddest moments, it struck me how different my life was with Devon in it. The way he kept me off-balance should have annoyed me. Instead, I saw our relationship as a mystery, something to continually unwrap. Having that element of mystery allowed me to keep my own secrets. Not that mine came even close to his.

I tiptoed to the pocket door, then carefully slid it open, assuming I'd catch several grown women eavesdropping. Lucky for them I anticipated their antics as they almost tumbled into the room. I shook my head, smiled, and stepped between Matilda and Hope to head back toward the sofa.

I joined Dani, who attempted to get something decent to watch on TV.

"How about Netflix? We've got Wi-Fi." I had a few movies in mind that would entertain.

"Oh, let's stream that reality bridal show about shopping for wedding dresses," Matilda said, bubbling over with excitement.

"You're not still on the marriage kick, are you?" I tried to add a little humor in my voice, but I worried that if catching up with Trey didn't work out, she'd want to follow through on her idea of finding someone online.

Matilda smirked. "Not for me, silly, for you!"

I should have known better. Once again, they were trying to interfere with my life.

"Yes, dear. No time like the present to plan," Prudence said from the front.

"It can take months, even years, Pip. We need to get started." My mom had already grabbed the remote from Dani and had started flipping channels.

"Ladies. I am not engaged." I held up my ringless hand as evidence and squashed the sudden lump I felt in my chest. "Devon and I aren't in that phase yet. We're still in phase two, you know, the committed but don't rock the boat phase."

"A girl can hope, Pip. After all, your sister kind of cheated us from our moment," my mom said.

"Babs and Tom had a beautiful wedding. They just chose to keep it simple and elegant." *Rather than tacky and raucous.* When Babs announced she was getting married, the ladies went into overdrive to plan the most elaborate wedding anyone in Luckland had ever imagined. Babs, however, while she appreciated lavish and elegant events, did not appreciate over the top. She nixed the live eighties tribute band, the taco bar, and the disco ball. Instead, she opted for a lovely garden wedding. Picture perfect, with a cellist performing during the ceremony and a small live band during the reception.

"Let's be clear, shall we? Devon and I have only been together a few months, so dress ogling right now is premature."

"You've known that boy your whole life, Pip, a few months? Pshaw!" Pru declared from her position in the driver's seat.

Pshaw? I had no idea where she got that stuff.

"Regardless, there are no plans for nuptials at the moment." Though I considered my relationship with Devon permanent, matrimony was not an institution I wanted to contemplate. My mother and father had such a strange marriage that I'd developed an aversion to the idea. I simply could not understand how two people who clearly loved each other would choose to live apart. If that was what marriage meant, I preferred to stay unwed.

There was an awkward silence, and by the looks on the

women's faces, they knew something I didn't, and I wasn't going to like it.

"What? Out with it."

More silence. I looked at Dani, my rock. My support. My compadre. Even she had that look. My suspicions grew. Like Pinocchio's nose.

"Dani, what exactly did you and Simon do today?" Normally, she would have told me because we told each other everything, but she shook her head and dragged her fingers across her lips. Indicating she was zipping them closed.

I stared at my mom, seated on the other side of me, then gazed at the other women. They all mimicked Dani's zipping gesture, confirming my worst fears. There was a surprise coming my way. So, I did what anyone would in the face of impending doom—I poured myself another daiquiri and sucked it down. The risk of brain freeze was nothing compared to the fear of what these ladies, and perhaps Devon, had in mind.

CHAPTER FIFTEEN

I awoke with a jolt, realizing the magic bus had come to a stop.

Dani and I had opened the sofa into a rather cozy bed, and while Pru had continued driving into the night, the rest of the posse had gone to their bunks.

Evidently, Pru had decided enough was enough, and she'd parked somewhere. I pulled apart the window blinds. It was pitch black out. From what I could see, we were in a parking lot, which I assumed was some sort of RV park. Dani and I had been so distracted we forgot to suggest a place for this beast to land.

I sighed. The motion of the bus had lulled me to sleep, but now I was awake, going back to sleep would not be an easy task. Without Devon sleeping beside me, insomnia ruled my life.

I checked my phone and found a text from him. Just a heart. I smiled and closed my eyes, then spent the next hour or so contemplating my future with Devon and how it might play out.

Eventually, I drifted off.

The next time I woke, it was to the tantalizing aroma of coffee and a heavy dose of cinnamon. Daylight had arrived, and we were moving again. I glanced out the window just in time to see an exit sign to I-10 West. I still had no idea where we were headed, but that little tidbit of information might be useful. I stretched, yawned, and reached out just as Marcy, who was at the counter fixing something for breakfast, handed me a mug filled with my morning elixir.

I carefully sipped my coffee and gave Dani a nudge. That girl could sleep through anything. Always could. She opened one eye.

"Time?"

"Time to rise and shine, Dani girl!"

"Coffee!" She made grabby hands, and Marcy handed her a mug before heading off to join the others at what I assumed was a game of cards. "Fab!" Dani sighed after a good long sip, then she leaned close to me so we could talk quietly. "So, any news on where we're headed?"

"I saw a sign for I-10 West, though I'm not sure where that will lead us."

Dani frowned and grabbed her phone. After a few minutes she gasped then held out her phone to me. She'd opened a page that mentioned a big festival in Tucson. I raised an eyebrow at her, and she mimed for me to keep looking, so I scrolled through the page, reading a list of the bands.

Mullet Madness arrives! Don't miss tonight's festival, to be held at the casino amphitheater!

Adam's Ants, The Policemen, U3, Guns and Rolaids, UB60, and the legendary lounge lizard himself, *Jon Von Jobi.*

I handed Dani her phone, jumped up, and ran into the Lovely Lavatory, which was the sign on the door, where I took deep breaths, bent over, hands on my knees, and tried not to squeal with laughter. Mullet Madness indeed! Once I was able to gain control, I texted Devon.

Me: Tucson. Big, big show tonight.

Devon: {Wink emoji}

Wink? Hmmm. Devon and Simon were way ahead of us. My guess? They were already on their way, which meant Devon had probably tracked my phone again. However, I didn't know whether they would show themselves or Devon would surprise Matilda. That was when I remembered it was the *big day*. Gathering my wits, I calmly went back up front.

"Happy Birthday, Matilda!" I said with as much gusto and peppiness as I could muster. She looked up and smiled.

"Thank you." Then she went back to her cards.

It seemed we were all going to downplay the occasion. I didn't have a problem with that, but everyone was awfully subdued. The atmosphere remained that way as we continued our journey. It seemed the party was over, at least for the time being.

As we approached Tucson, we didn't turn off where I expected. "Wasn't that our exit? We just passed the sign for the casino. Isn't that where we're headed?" I suddenly remembered I wasn't supposed to know. Hopefully, they assumed I had guessed our destination based on the last time I went on a road trip with the ladies, where we ended up at a casino.

"Oh, eventually, Pip, but their RV parking is horrible. We're headed up to a wonderful spot by Picacho Peak. Perfect for you to take some photos," Prudence said from the front.

"It would be perfect *if* I had my camera."

"Never fear, Pip, we've got you covered." Tillie reached into one of the overhead bins and pulled down an unopened box containing a very new Nikon D500 with built-in Wi-Fi and Bluetooth. That was a seriously amazing and expensive piece of equipment. "Will this do?" she asked.

"You keep one of these around for what purpose?"

"Why for you, sweetie," my mom said. "You can't travel without a camera."

"Well, can I just say thank you, bless you, and you'll all forever be my favorite women?" This was my dream camera. I had just replaced my old one because someone had stolen it when they'd broken into my house. My new camera was good, but this?

"Don't thank us," said Hope. "It was Devon's idea."

Devon had bought me a top-of-the-line Nikon and stored it on the RV on the off chance I'd find myself on an unplanned trip aboard the luxury liner? The man had some serious intuitive mojo. He was also the best boyfriend ever. I was now in photo geek heaven, even if I didn't have my hiking gear. Heck, I didn't even have a change of clothes. Dani and I slept in some old t-shirts my mom handed us, which we still wore.

"Mom, love the camera, but what are Dani and I supposed to wear today? I mean, we didn't come prepared for this. What-ever this is..."

Right on cue, Marcy came strutting down the aisle with shopping bags. From the mall. She sat down beside me and began pulling things out.

Some of the items were ones Dani and I had hastily left behind in the dressing room, like our sexy little outfits, which were not appropriate for a day hike, but Marcy also pulled out jeans, tube socks, long-sleeve shirts, and layering tops. So, the women seemed to have planned for the unknown eventuality that we'd be headed this way.

CHAPTER SIXTEEN

Where we landed at Picacho Peak billed itself as a resort community for those over fifty-five, as well as an RV park. They had pickleball, shuffleboard, and lots of golf carts. I gave them bonus points for the ostrich ranch next door.

We'd pulled up to a lovely home site with a double-wide manufactured home and an SUV in the driveway. Much to Dani's and my surprise, but not the women's, the fully furnished house had a stocked refrigerator and a gassed-up car, ready to go—as if someone had prepped it all in advance. I'd learned to stop asking questions that inevitably went unanswered, so Dani and I simply changed into hiking clothes, grabbed our supplies and the car keys, and left. We had much to discuss, and a little privacy would help.

"What are we missing, Dani? How did the ladies know we'd end up here? How could they know Trey would be a no-show in Denver?"

Dani pursed her lips and tapped on the steering wheel. "I don't think they did. They all turned up to see him in Denver, and only when they saw the poster did they turn around and jump on the RV."

"So, this is their plan B in case something went south in Denver, which they somehow predicted." I shook my head. "Those damn Tarot cards they're always playing with. Do you think they actually work to some degree?"

"I don't know. But the women often show mystical powers of some sort, don't they?" Dani sounded as sure as I felt, so I decided we'd have to keep an eye on the Luckland Ladies' supernatural activities moving forward.

We pulled into the state park a few minutes later and got ourselves situated, marking off our mental checklist for supplies consisting of water, cellphone power packs, snacks, and my fantastic new camera. My next blog post was already forming in my head—until I realized it was mid-autumn. I wouldn't find a single flowering succulent anywhere. I ended up taking scenic panoramas rather than close-up blooms.

The wind picked up suddenly, and the sky darkened to the north. Something was headed our way. Whether it was rain or dust, I couldn't yet tell. Regardless, it was time to go. We quickly gathered our things, headed back down, and packed up the car, but one look in the rearview mirror as we got on the highway told me we were in trouble. A haboob—a massive dust storm that could be miles wide and black out an entire city—was right behind us. We needed to pull off the road and wait for the storm to pass. Unfortunately, there was only a shallow culvert running alongside the emergency lane, which wasn't far enough off the roadway to help, but we couldn't stay where we were. With no choice, I turned the wheel and hoped for the best. We bounced pretty hard in the ditch and ended up in the field alongside it. At least we were now far enough off the road not to get hit by a semi when the sky went black.

Dani reached over as I turned off the engine and gripped my hand.

"We got this," she said.

I'd never been inside a dust storm before. I knew we needed to brace for dust to coat the vehicle and possibly get in the car. However, I was more terrified of a vehicle wiping out on the interstate, flying off the road, and crashing on top of us like in those viral videos.

"You know, it would be just my luck to land the perfect boyfriend then die in a freaking pile of dirt," I commented as the wind outside picked up and debris started flying.

"You? I haven't even *found* mine yet, though Simon has some serious potential," she said with a laugh.

"How can you laugh?" My voice was loud and panicky. I squeezed her hand as things started banging against the SUV and the swirling dirt got thicker and grittier. Visibility was zero, though blaring horns and the horrific crunch of metal on metal filtered through the roar of the wind.

"I wonder how long storms like these last," I said after a particularly loud crash.

"I was trying to find out, but my phone has no signal," Dani muttered. "Well, crap."

Eventually, the buffeting wind stopped, and we found ourselves surrounded by an eerie silence.

We sat quietly, waiting for the darkness to ebb. However, with the filtered light came an entirely new problem. Several inches of gritty, sandy dirt buried us. If we tried to open the door, the detritus would likely flood the interior.

"Try the engine. If it starts, use the wipers," Dani suggested.

"Here goes nothing," I mumbled. When I turned the key, that was what we got. Nothing. Click. Click. Click. Dead as a doornail.

"Got another idea?" I asked ruefully.

"How about the emergency button on your phone? Didn't you say it works even when you have no bars?"

"Yes, it uses GPS to signal Devon and let him know I'm in trouble. I think he's already tracking me and knows where I am, but it certainly won't hurt to push it." I grabbed my phone and hit the handy dandy Devon to the rescue button.

"Remember the time we swam out to the big rock in the lake and were too tired to swim back?" Dani suddenly asked.

"We pretended we were shipwrecked." I chuckled as I remembered our adventure. We couldn't have been more than eleven.

"Do you remember how we were rescued?" Dani spoke quietly, a question in her voice.

I thought for a moment. "Devon. It was Devon. He swam out with the inner tube to fetch us." I'd forgotten.

"And the time we went out with those freakazoid twins? They drove us out to that deserted shack and wouldn't bring us home."

"God, they were jerks, weren't they?"

"Yeah, of course, but how did we get home?" Dani was headed down memory lane now.

"Devon happened along," I murmured. "Just happened to be driving out that way."

"There's one more thing, Pip. Something I swore I'd never repeat." Dani exhaled as if what she was about to impart would be important to me.

"Out with it. I'm a big girl. I can take it." I honestly wasn't sure what she would say, and I wasn't nearly as confident as my statement.

"Harley James."

"That total prick? What about him?" Just the name made me shudder. Captain of the football team and charming as a diamondback snake. However, at sixteen, I'd been naïve as hell and totally crushing on him. He'd asked me to prom, then stood me up. I'd sat on my front stoop for hours. Dressed up with nowhere to go. That night, I'd cried myself to sleep.

"After school, the day of prom, I had to drop off a box of decorations in the gym. When I got there, the door was locked, so I went around to the back door, figuring it might be open. As I got close, I heard voices, then yelling and a scuffle. I hurried closer and saw Devon and Harley rolling around on the ground. Harley had a bloody nose. When they saw me, Harley got up and ran. I asked Devon what had happened. He knew I'd go to Tillie if he didn't tell me. Plus, he had a gash above his eye."

"Wait, the little scar above his eye? That wasn't falling off his bike?"

"Nope."

"Out with it, Dani." Whatever she said next would change how I viewed my past life with Devon. I hoped in a good way. My whole romantic trajectory had changed that night. No one got stood up for prom and remained unscathed.

"Devon overheard Harley bragging to his buddies. Said he was going to 'bang you' after prom. That you were an easy mark. He said they all laughed, and there was a betting pool. Pippa, I'm so sorry... I never told you because you didn't deserve to live with knowing those assholes did that."

"At least he didn't stand me up. However, going with him to the prom could have been worse. I always knew there was something totally off about him asking me." Tears filled my eyes, but I didn't know whether from dust or pent-up repressed memories.

Dani took my hand. "Devon waited until Harley's friends took off, then jumped him. I supposed Devon used some of those moves we learned in self-defense classes. Anyway, he told me if I breathed a word to anyone, especially you, he'd deny it and tell my parents about my sneaking out and every other house rule I broke."

Nothing was ever as it seemed in Luckland, and my high school tragedy was just another shining example. Devon to the rescue was a thing long before I recognized it. If I hadn't already given my heart to Devon, I would have right then because the only person who could break it would never do anything but protect it.

CHAPTER SEVENTEEN

"Pippa! Dani! You in there?"

Devon. I'd never felt so relieved in my life.

"We're okay. Just get us out, would you?" Dani yelled.

"Scoot to the center in case anything shatters. We're going to clear off the dirt before we open the door." That sounded like Simon.

"Got it!" Turning to Dani, I grinned. "How soon after we left Denver did they follow?"

"Probably as soon as they could, for which I'm grateful. Otherwise, we could have been stuck in here for hours."

Little by little, the guys cleared off the dirt, allowing rays of light to peek through the glass. The whole situation felt totally surreal, so I grabbed my camera and captured a few shots, just enough for a fun little blog post. Maybe I'd title it *The Clearing* or *Rays of Hope,* as that was the feeling the images evoked.

Trying to get a better angle for the perfect composition, I leaned against my door, and it suddenly opened. It wouldn't take a brain surgeon to realize where I'd ended up—ass first on the ground. Devon stood over me, hands on hips, eyebrows raised, and a half-grin on his face.

"Do I even want to know?" he asked in that low, husky, sex-on-a-stick voice.

"Nope, you most certainly don't." I laughed and held out my hand.

He pulled me up and was about to greet me *properly* when I noticed Dani and Simon standing face to face, staring at each other. Intriguing.

"They'll have to tow the car. You can ride with us to the RV park," Devon said.

"How do you know we're staying at the RV park?"

"I'd tell you, Pip, but honestly, I kind of like keeping you guessing." Devon laughed, kissed me, and tugged me back toward the highway. Now the air had cleared, the tracks where we went off the road were visible, and I shivered. A few feet left or right and we might have been cactus food. Or worse.

The boys drove a rented SUV with an Arizona plate, and the drive to the RV park only took a couple of minutes—which meant we had almost made it back before the cataclysmic dirt devil overtook Dani and me.

Pulling in, it seemed awfully quiet around the house. The RV was there, so the ladies had to be around somewhere. We walked in through the slightly open front door. Total silence greeted us.

"Hello?" I called out.

"Mom?" Dani yelled right after me.

"Mother dearest?" That was Devon.

Simon kept his mouth shut.

Nothing.

"Well, they couldn't have gone far," Devon said.

"Maybe they're playing mini-golf or at the pool. Come on, let's go look around."

We didn't get two steps out the door when screams filled the air. We all started running. Devon and Simon took the lead, which was good since I couldn't tell where the screams came from. It felt as if we ran through an RV maze.

Zipping past an Airstream trailer, I caught a glimpse of classic Americana. Mesh-weave beach chairs, probably from the sixties, sat out front. Their occupants? I mentally called them Stan and Marge. He was a little over the hill with a truly overstated toupee. She had a little too much hair color and a little too much mascara. Between the two of them sat a little tiny folding table with a cocktail shaker. I was definitely coming back later with my camera.

After a frantic few minutes of searching, we caught sight of the ladies huddled together in front of a large tour bus. Not quite the luxury liner we'd traveled in, more of a beat-up older model RV with painted lettering on the side with half the letters missing.

Devon pushed his way through to get to Tillie. The other ladies held her up, and they all appeared to be in shock.

"Mom? What's going on?" He looked over his shoulder at Simon, who stood by the open door to the bus. Waiting for the ladies to respond, Devon nodded toward Simon, signaling him to enter.

"Ladies, can you please tell me what Simon is about to find in that bus?" Devon used his *I'm the law* voice. They all turned to look at him, but not one of them spoke. I worried they'd gone too far in one of their schemes.

"Dev," Simon called from the doorway of the bus. "You'd better take a look."

CHAPTER EIGHTEEN

Devon and Simon's voices were too low to make out what they were saying, and the bus's windows were too high for me to see inside.

"Dani, give me a lift." I offered her a foot, waiting for her to cup her hands and boost me up. It had been a long time since we'd done such a maneuver, but it was a skill like riding a bike, not forgotten and handy to have.

I got just enough height to peer in the middle window. Devon and Simon crouched over something. Once Devon moved out of the way, what they were looking at came into view. Startled, I toppled back, taking Dani with me.

"What the eff?" Dani muttered as she brushed some dirt off her jeans.

"It's a body," I whispered. "Shh, listen."

"It's not him, thank god," Devon said. "Did you call it in?"

"Yeah," Simon replied.

"Not what we expected to find down here, eh?"

"I gotta tell ya, Devon. Nothing surprises me when it comes to your mom and those wacky women."

I chuckled softly. Simon nailed that one.

"Well, let's just hope they had nothing, and I mean nothing, to do with this. Sometimes, I think those women need a new hobby. You know, like baking? Quilting?" Devon's voice got louder with each suggestion.

"Perish the thought," my mom said.

"Hold up, ladies." Simon came down the steps as the women made their way over to the bus's door. "You can't go in there. Was he like that when you found him? Who found him?"

"We all did, Simon," Hope said immediately. "Tillie went first, then we heard her scream, and we all went in there to see."

"Tillie? I need you to tell me what you saw." Simon spoke quietly, but his tone was demanding. As Devon's often was.

Tillie was still sobbing, but she nodded. "A dead body. I saw a dead body. I thought it was Trey. It sounded like Trey."

"Wait, what? I thought you said this guy was dead when you found him."

"Yes, yes, dear boy, quite dead. But we came over here when we heard singing."

"And you thought it was Trey. Trey Marks?" Devon asked as he came down the steps.

"Yes. Nobody sings *It's My Life* like Trey does. When I got here, it was silent, no more singing, so I knocked on the door. When nobody answered, I might have, you know, pushed it to see if it would open."

"And?"

"It did, so I went in. And there it was."

"Look, the sheriff is on the way, so nobody goes anywhere. Dani and Pip, why don't you go back to the house to grab some water and whatever the ladies might need while we wait here." Devon was all business. I supposed dead bodies required that.

Dani and I went off on our task, and once we delivered everything, we hung next to the women, trying to be unobtrusive. Seems we weren't unobtrusive enough.

"You two are not the primary witnesses, so it would be better for everyone if you left," Devon said to Dani and me.

I wanted to argue, but by the look in Devon's eyes, I wouldn't win. "Okay, but just tell us one thing. Whose bus is it?"

"Don't know that yet."

I had an idea it might belong to a band starring in the Mullet Madness festival. I grabbed Dani's arm, and we turned to go. Not that I had any intention of really leaving. I was sure we could find a little nook to hide out in.

"And, Pip?" Devon called after me as Dani and I slowly walked away.

"Yes, dear?"

"Do not hide behind the nearest RV. Go to the house. Go inside the house. Stay inside the house. And lock the door."

Ugh. Once again, Dani and I were forced to miss all the good stuff. Though that last bit about locking the door reminded me there could be a murderer on the loose. I decided to look in the closets and under the beds before trying to relax. When darkness fell, and no one had returned, we stayed busy fixing sandwiches, making sure there'd be plenty to eat when they all got back.

"Pip. Do you think our lives are abnormal? I always thought of us as just average kids growing up in a typical small town. But lately, things have been...unusual."

"Dani, your father played pro ball, and your mother was a cover model. You grew up in the mountains yet train Navy SEALs in advanced diving. You're not average."

"Okay, but you were pretty normal," Dani said.

I had to disagree. "Nope. Not normal. My parents are next-door neighbors. *To each other!* What's normal about that? Devon grew up thinking his parents were missionaries who disappeared in the Congo." I paused for emphasis. "Stop me anytime you think I've strayed from normal, and let's not forget Luck-land's legendary gold that may actually turn out to be real. *And our illustrious ghosts. Shall I go on?"*

Dani laughed and shook her head. "No, my turn! We're sitting here in an RV park next door to an ostrich farm in Tucson, waiting for our moms to finish being interrogated after discovering a dead body in a bus they broke into."

I laughed too. Totally inappropriate under the circumstances, but these circumstances *were* ridiculous. I reached for the bottle of prosecco, then collapsed next to Dani on the couch before pouring us some refills.

Lifting our glasses, we clinked them together for a toast.

"To living a completely ridiculous life!"

"To sharing that completely ridiculous life with my best friend!"

"Girls! We're back," Matilda called out.

"Oh look, Kate, they've made us supper," Rosa commented from the kitchen.

Dani and I quickly hopped off the sofa to greet them.

As they began pulling the bar stools around the kitchen island where we'd laid out the sandwiches, Matilda spoke up. "Now, remember what Devon and Simon told us. We can't reveal anything that isn't public knowledge."

Dani and I shared a look.

"I think there's a rule that if more than four people know, it's public. Isn't that right?" I asked.

"I'm sure that's right," Hope said.

"Yeah, I'm sure that's right as well," I said. "Now spill. What happened after we left? Who was on the bus, and whose bus was it?"

"It was a musician's tour bus," my mother stated.

Ha, just as I thought.

"And the body?" Dani leaned in as she asked the key question.

My mom looked around the island before taking one of her dramatic pauses. "This goes no further, but...it appears to be a—"

The front door opened.

I groaned and shook my head. "Those two have the worst timing."

CHAPTER NINETEEN

THOUGH FRUSTRATED, I HAD TO SMILE WHEN DEVON SNUCK UP BEHIND me and put his hands on my shoulders to lean in for a kiss. He must have known he'd interrupted my interrogation. I could only hope I'd get some intel from him later.

"Why aren't you still at the scene?" I asked.

"The local police took over, so there was no longer any need for us to be there. We just stayed to keep an eye on the ladies."

"You seemed awfully chatty with one of the deputies," Matilda said.

"That was because I happened to mention you love Sedona, and it turned out he's got a place up there. Usually, it's rented out, but they had a last-minute cancellation. As it's your birthday, he said you can stay there for the next few days." Devon pulled out his phone and began scrolling until he found the link and handed me the phone. Wow. The photo showed huge floor-to-ceiling windows with the sunset reflected off the spectacular red rock mesas and buttes of Sedona. I gave the phone to Dani, who quickly scanned it before passing it to Matilda.

"So, the police are going to let us leave?" I asked. "Well,

Dani and me, for sure, but the rest of them?" I nodded toward the women all hovering over Devon's phone.

"The police have a person or two of interest. So, you're all off the hook for now," Simon said. "You can go anywhere you want. Just stay out of trouble."

I pulled Devon a few steps from the others. "What about the festival," I whispered, not wanting the women to hear.

"It's been called off."

"Do they know that?" I indicated the women again.

"Yes. After we discovered who the bus belonged to, most of the acts got put on the suspect list. The local police are trying to trace them all."

"Including your dad?" I couldn't believe Trey Marks would be involved, but then, I didn't know him.

Devon sighed and nodded. "Including my dad."

"I'm sorry."

"It's fine. There's no point in worrying about it until we learn more."

I moved into his arms to hug him. Matilda had yet to find out her long-lost love was supposed to perform at the festival, but Devon had held on to the hope of seeing him for quite some time. Devon planted a kiss on my forehead, then smiled.

"So, are you going to Sedona with them?" he asked.

"Well, someone still has to keep an eye on them. What about you?"

"There are a few things Simon and I want to check on. Then we'll see."

All the women voted to go to Sedona, so after a brief and somewhat rushed goodbye to Devon and Simon, the rest of us ended up back in the Luxmobile, as I decided to call it, and we headed for the spiritual mecca of the world. I wanted to ask Matilda more about the body, but before I had a chance, she took center stage, so to speak.

"I know all of you have been keeping something from me, so come on, fess up. I heard Trey on that bus. I would know that voice anywhere. What is going on?"

"Oh, Tillie dear. We do have some explaining to do, I suppose." Hope looked sheepish.

"You *suppose*?" Matilda replied with a scowl.

"Tillie, sweetie, it was your birthday surprise," Marcy said softly. "Trey was supposed to be the opening act in Denver, but when we arrived, it seemed he'd canceled."

"Unfortunately, it's happened before. That birthday bash in Boulder? A freak snowstorm killed that one," said my mom.

Marcy smiled. "Oh yes, and what about that time in Disneyland?"

"Disneyland?" Matilda looked bewildered.

"That trip was supposed to end with a Trey Marks concert that never happened because it seemed he succumbed to food poisoning," Hope said with a shake of her head. "Never eat deviled eggs in the green room."

Then all the ladies started talking at once, adding their versions of what had happened in the past. I shook my head, hardly able to believe they'd traveled all around the country without me knowing. Until recently, I hadn't even known they'd stepped outside Colorado. These women continued to surprise me at every turn.

"So, Tucson was plan B because every time you've tried to pin Trey down, he's never been in the place you originally planned, correct?" I asked, wanting to get everything clear in my head.

My mom nodded. "We've tried so hard over the years, and we didn't want to take the chance of missing him again. This time, we found out he was supposed to be in Denver *and* Tucson. So, we made two plans to cover our bases."

"So, all this was for me? For my birthday? Trying to get Trey and me back together?" Matilda asked.

"I think that about sums it up," I said.

"Well, aren't you all the best friends I could ever have?" She sniffed, then tears started flowing. Not just from Matilda. They all started sniffling and hugging each other.

I could only think how I would react if my best friend gave me a dead body for my birthday.

"This calls for a celebration," Rosa said as she opened the fridge and pulled out a bottle of prosecco. She also brought out the sandwiches we hadn't eaten, which they'd packed up to bring along.

The rest of the drive went smoothly. Surprisingly, we didn't even hit traffic through Phoenix. Sadly, our nighttime arrival meant we would miss the spectacular views that would normally greet us. Sedona was known for its shock and awe scenery. The Red Rock mountains that rose above the desert were amazing. I looked forward to spending a few days hiking and photographing it all. The others wouldn't mind if I headed off on my own as they were all busy planning their mini-vacation—complete with mystics, vortexes, and psychics, of which I wanted no part.

We arrived and, to our delight, discovered the house was palatial, with half a dozen bedrooms and floor-to-ceiling windows to enjoy the view. I briefly wondered how a sheriff's deputy could afford a house like that. I checked the rates online, and at five hundred dollars a night for rentals, I supposed they could. It certainly commanded that price. Every bedroom had an en suite bath, a large-screen TV, and outdoor access to a balcony or patio. The main floor included a sunken living room with a wet bar, a dining room, and a massive chef's kitchen. Pretty damn spectacular.

Just as we were about to divvy up the rooms, my phone buzzed.

Devon: Grab the master.

Me: What? Where are you?

Devon: Be there in an hour.

I should have known. At least he told me instead of sneaking into the house and terrifying us all—which would be just like him. I was glad, of course. An awesome place like Sedona should be spent with someone special, which prompted me to wonder if he was alone.

Me: Is Simon with you?

Devon: Affirmative.

Me: And where is he sleeping?

Devon: TBD.

I grinned. Typical Devon.

"Okay, ladies, it seems our favorite boys are on their way. So how about I take that lovely master suite." I figured the assumptive approach was best.

"But of course, Pip. Dani, why don't you take that guest suite in the front. The girls and I will take the upstairs quarters," Prudence announced. By the look on her face, Dani and I could tell she figured Simon would sleep downstairs. And not on the couch.

Dani laughed. "Aunt Pru, we're not there yet."

"Well, what the hell are you waiting for, girl? Life's too short," Prudence replied with a shake of her head.

Rosa frowned. "Pru, that's my baby girl you're talking to. I'd prefer not to have this discussion."

Uh-oh. Time for a distraction. Thankfully, Marcy had one planned.

"All right, girls, butts down on the floor, Tarot time."

CHAPTER TWENTY

"Isn't it a bit late for that?" Aside from my aversion to the supernatural—ghost sightings included, Devon and Simon would arrive soon, and I had no idea what Marcy had in mind.

"Won't take long. I can feel the energy. This house is perfectly situated in the vortex," Marcy replied.

"Care to explain for those of us not well-versed in all things supernatural?" Dani asked.

"Mystical, Dani, not supernatural," Hope said, always a stickler for words.

"Very well, mystical. Explain." I was just as curious as Dani.

Marcy smiled. "All right, back in the day, there was a wonderful medium whose name escapes me who discovered that Sedona has a unique energy. Something Native Americans have long known. You can renew and revitalize your chi by tapping into that energy."

"As opposed to Luckland's energy?" I asked. They often spoke about tapping into the Native American magic in and around Luckland and using it to hold back the spirits when they did their annual Founders' Day ritual.

"That's a different type of energy," Prudence said.

All the ladies shared a look—one I'd become familiar with. They were hiding something.

"Circling back to Tarot, how does this vortex help?" Dani asked.

"Sit down, and we'll show you," Matilda said. "I have a question."

We all sat in a circle while Marcy did some sort of shuffling technique with the cards. Not the way I shuffle, but more of a sifting. Then she held the deck in one palm and had Matilda place her palm over it.

"Okay, Tillie, go ahead and ask."

"Is it our time?"

I had no idea what she meant, but the ladies all nodded as if they understood Matilda's question.

Marcy dealt out five cards and laid them out in a cross pattern. She studied them carefully, then nodded. "Yes. But, Tillie, there will be doubt. Regret. You will need to summon your courage and face it head-on. Then you will have what you desire."

Again, all the ladies nodded and murmured, smiling now.

I waited for an explanation, but it didn't seem as if any was forthcoming. "Obviously, you all have some higher level of understanding than Dani or me. Care to share?"

Marcy nodded. "Let me explain. You see, each card tells us something." Pointing at the bottom card, she smiled. "This is The Moon. It tells us right now there is uncertainty and a bit of illusion, which in this case, means all is not as it seems."

"And this one?" I pointed to the top card.

"Not so fast. Over here." She pointed to the center card. "The Two of Cups. This is desire. Clearly, Matilda is seeking her other half. Over here is the Wheel of Fortune. This means there are positive energies toward success. The Ten of Wands is providing a challenge, telling us someone is carrying a heavy load, which they must overcome."

"And the top card?" Dani asked. "Looks like a good one to me."

"The Lovers. If all the challenges are met, and the desire is there, this will be her fate."

Matilda faced me. "Pip, honey, we all know what I'm asking for. But I guess the answer isn't that clear. I think we should head into town tomorrow. We need to see Lali."

"Lali?" That was a name I'd not heard before.

"She's a psychic reader, works out of the crystal shop we frequent."

"Wait. Stop right there. The crystal shop you *frequent*? How often do you come here?" I was flabbergasted—and a little concerned when nobody responded to my question.

"Never mind that, Pippa," my mom finally said. "The point is, we need to go to town tomorrow and see her. She'll know what to do next."

"I agree," Marcy said. "Just looking at these cards, there's something else we need to know. I'm concerned about The Moon. We need to sort through that."

"What needs sorting through?"

We all whipped our heads around at the sound of Devon's voice. They shouldn't have arrived yet. Worse, we didn't hear them come in.

"Nothing to worry about, boys. Now, come in and tell us everything you learned." Matilda sounded quite chipper, considering.

"Who's the stiff?" Prudence waved a hand in the direction of Tucson. She'd been laying off the booze lately but apparently had decided to indulge a little.

"The victim remains unidentified," Simon said. "But we'll find out soon enough."

"Back to that sorting through comment," Devon said. "What are you girls up to? Haven't you gotten into enough mischief?"

"Don't be silly, Devon." Hope stood, then headed into the kitchen. "Now come along. We saved you some supper, which you need to hurry up and eat so we can, you know…"

"Know what?" he whispered as he followed her close behind.

I wasn't sure what she said after that, but I had a hunch it involved celebrating Matilda's birthday. Poor girl. Instead of meeting her long-lost troubadour, she'd met a corpse. Not what I'd call a happy kind of day.

Sure enough, Hope and Marcy hadn't failed to deliver in the cake department. I guessed they had it in the freezer of the RV. A spectacular three-layer chocolate mocha mousse cake. With a male figurine candle on top. In his birthday suit. It was worth it just to see the looks on Devon and Simon's faces.

The ladies' rendition of Happy Birthday, a la Marilyn Monroe, was amazing and hilarious. After which, they all got into their own birthday suits to enjoy the hot tub out on the patio with a bottle of champagne. It was getting pretty late by then, so Dani, Simon, Devon, and I relaxed in front of the TV, where I immediately grabbed the remote and turned on the hit new series, Indian Matchmaking.

"Pip, what is this?" Devon's gaze was glued to the TV, and he looked ready to burst.

"Don't judge until you've watched it." I leaned up and kissed his cheek, then got comfy. When I snuggled up to Devon, it didn't matter what was on TV. Somehow, he centered me, and I needed some of that Devon magic after a day from hell as we'd had. I laid my head against Devon's shoulder and closed my eyes, the soft sounds of his breathing lulling me to sleep.

I awoke on the couch. Dani lay curled up in the corner of the other sofa. The boys had vanished. The dark house was silent while dawn's colors began to reflect off the red rocks outside. I checked my phone, knowing the first clue to whatever had gone wrong would be there.

Devon: Sorry, had to run. Stay out of trouble.

What was that supposed to mean? It deserved a witty response though.

Me: Does the male revue count as trouble?

I couldn't resist. Teasing Devon always entertained.

CHAPTER TWENTY-ONE

"Have you been to a reading before, Pippa?" Lali asked after I settled in the small but comfortable room and sat in a lounge-style chair.

When the ladies had dragged Dani and me into the Crystal Catalyst, gemstones, rocks, pendants, and crystals of every sort surrounded us. Matilda had introduced Dani and me to Lali, who Matilda said was her psychic. Lali had then taken Matilda straight to the back room while Dani and I browsed. I had scanned the brochure on the counter and learned Lali was born Leland a half-century ago and raised in Oklahoma among the Cherokee. Leland moved to Sedona a decade ago and revealed Lali to the world. Stunningly beautiful, I wanted to take photos the minute I saw her. She was magnetic and flamboyant, but whether or not she truly was a psychic had yet to be determined.

"Can't say I have."

"Well, it's important to understand that we all have our own spirit guides, but they aren't always who we think they are. You need to expect the unexpected."

I wasn't convinced. When Matilda returned from her reading, she was all smiles. Before I had a chance to comment, Lali ushered me into the back room and told me to sit down. I'd watched enough psychic medium shows to be leery, but as I didn't want to offend Lali, I decided I'd play along.

"Let's start with why you're here."

"Because Matilda dragged me in?" I smiled, hoping Lali would know I was just kidding.

"Hmm. Well, we'll start with the easy stuff." She tipped her head and appeared to contemplate. "You're a photographer. A people watcher. You study them."

Matilda could have told Lali that, but I let her continue, expecting her to say something about my love life, perhaps that I'd found my one and only. I supposed it wouldn't hurt to get *some* affirmation—even a mystical one.

"There is something I don't quite understand. I see a house of cards. Normally, it represents an area of your life that you have no control over. But in this case, I feel as if it's literally a house."

"Anything else?" I asked, confused.

"You have a path to choose. Be careful. Choose the wrong path, and you won't end where you want to be."

"How will I know which is the right path?"

"How does anyone know? You have to do what's best for you."

Well, then. That was clear as mud. I left the back room no wiser than before I'd entered.

No one else felt the need for a reading, so we headed to lunch and ordered a round of margaritas and nachos.

"So, what did Lali say?" Dani asked after our drinks and food arrived.

"She said I was a photographer, and I had a path to choose, but I had to make sure I chose the right path, or I wouldn't end up where I wanted to be."

"I bet you get a job offer photographing the Alaskan wilderness. You'd have to leave. Break Devon's heart," Pru announced, tipping her glass for emphasis as she nodded knowingly.

"Gee, thanks, Prudence. That sure eases my mind," I muttered

"Don't pay her any mind, dear," my mother said. "I am fairly certain I know what your choice will be."

"And?" I asked.

"And what, dear?" Her smile didn't make me feel any better.

Matilda shook her head. "Pip, you make choices every day. I'm sure Lali was just saying to be mindful when you make big decisions."

I'd already made the biggest decision of my life by letting Devon *into* my life. I couldn't see another big decision on the horizon, except what color to decorate our new bedroom at the — "Oh, crapola! The house!"

"What house? Your house?" Dani asked.

I nodded. "Lali mentioned a house of cards, but she said it was a real house. Just now..." I swallowed. "Something is going on at Mystic Manor."

Matilda jumped up. "Let's go, girls. We've got to get back home."

"Pippa, you should have mentioned the house of cards earlier," Marcy whispered. "That explains everything."

Maybe to Marcy, but not to me. I didn't even understand what made me think there was something wrong at the Manor, except the moment I'd thought of the house, a chill had slithered down my spine. Now I was the one with some explaining to do, and Devon might be a harder sell. Especially by text.

Me: Emergency. Headed home.

Devon: What? Wait, I'm coming.

Me: The crazy train is leaving the station. See you at MM.

Devon: Please be careful. I'll call you tonight. Don't talk to strangers.

The last text was a little odd, but nothing out of character. We headed back to the house, gathered anything we'd left inside, locked it back up, and piled onto the RV. Destination Luckland.

I supposed our frazzled mini vacay wasn't too bad all in all. Matilda seemed to take her birthday adventures all in stride—until we were well on our way and turned on the satellite TV to see Trey Marks's photo staring back at us with a banner reading *'wanted in connection with body found at RV park'* scrolling across the screen. That sent her over the edge.

CHAPTER TWENTY-TWO

I don't think Matilda had ever sounded so anguished. I watched her fume as she put the call on speaker and paced up and down the Luxmobile.

"Mom, please. Calm yourself. It isn't what you think, but I am not at liberty to discuss it."

"Your own father? What could you be thinking?" She continued muttering about loyalties and betrayal until Devon finally cut in.

"Go home, Mom, and do not, I repeat, do not do anything until I get there." Devon also sounded pretty ticked off. I'd never heard the two of them use that tone with each other, but I understood where they were coming from. Neither wanted to think Trey was involved in a man's death, and I agreed, but there must have been a reason why Trey had been singled out and plastered all over the news.

"Tillie, hang up. Let's discuss this rationally." Hope, ever the peacemaker, disconnected the call. Rosa put her arm around Matilda, nudging her over to the little banquette, and with both hands on her shoulders, pushed her down into the window seat. Prudence pulled off at the next exit, so she could also join her sisters-in-misery at the table.

Dani and I were torn. We trusted Devon and Simon. Mostly. And we trusted the ladies. Somewhat. Faith versus reality was a balancing act. We figured the best course of action was to just stay out of whatever the ladies were up to.

We pulled up in front of my house close to midnight. Dani and I knew the women were off to cause trouble, but there was nothing we could do, so we grabbed our things, waved them goodbye, and headed inside. We were exhausted, and I needed sleep to prepare for whatever hell we had to face in the morning.

I woke in heaven, wrapped in Devon's arms. He had to have been awfully quiet for me not to notice when he came home. I rolled over to study him. Unable to help myself, I slipped out of his arms, then grabbed my phone from the nightstand to snap a picture. I had no intention of sharing the photo with anyone— it was just for me. Sleeping Devon was a sight to behold. The tips of his long and inky black eyelashes rested on his cheeks when he slept. I sighed, snapped one more picture, then leaned over to give him a quick kiss, only jumping a foot or so when he pulled me into a deeper, more satisfying one.

"Morning, Red," he whispered.

"Good morning, Detective." I smiled. "Coffee?"

"You stay. I'll get it."

"Not this time. You stay, and I'll get it."

He grinned. "This will cost me, won't it?"

"Absolutely!" I laughed, then scurried off the bed to head to the shower, relaxed and looking forward to a nice, calm breakfast where we could maybe have a pleasant chat and get some answers.

In the kitchen, I sipped my coffee and enjoyed the view as Devon started on breakfast. Simon sat on the couch and stretched his arms over his head. I had knocked on Dani's door on the way to the kitchen, figuring she'd make her way down eventually.

Everything seemed normal until the rap on the front door. I debated answering it, but Devon looked at me, brows raised.

"Okay, I'll get it, but if it's the mystical matriarchs, I'm not letting them in."

I opened the door, expecting the posse. Instead, I found Deputy Martin O'Hara.

"May I come in, Pip? Here to see your boy."

My boy? Well, that was amusing. Martin was my dad's age, so I supposed Devon was a boy to him. It just sounded odd. Martin was in uniform, so I assumed this was official business and he wasn't out searching for Prudence. That would have had me worried. Seeing him in his official capacity wasn't too worrisome.

"Come on in. Can I get you some coffee? Just made it."

"That'd be great." He followed me into the kitchen.

"Morning, Marty. What can I do for you?" Devon asked as he handed the deputy a mug.

"Well, we had a few incidents over at your new place while you were gone. Thought maybe we ought to discuss them."

"I didn't hear about anything. Are we talking vandalism?" Devon frowned. I took the spatula out of his hand as he seemed to have forgotten he was scrambling eggs.

"On the surface, it might appear to be a jokester. There's no damage, but um, well... The whole crew disappeared. Tom called me last night and said every one of them quit. The crew from Denver left town entirely." Martin leaned against the counter, mimicking Devon. Arms crossed, mug in hand.

"What the hell happened?"

"According to Hunter Jackson, they claimed the place was haunted."

I paused my scrambling for a moment and looked at them. I hadn't forgotten about Lali's warning about Mystic Manor nor my spine-chilling reaction when I'd thought about the house, but I'd been too tired last night to do anything—not that I had any idea what I could do. "I think it *is* haunted," I said, remembering my ghostly apparitions and the flying rodent or whatever it was. "I mean, we live in Luckland. We're *supposed* to have ghosts."

"Haunted or not, it appears someone wanted no one working on the house. The question is why." Devon put his mug down, grabbed the spatula from me, and began serving up breakfast. I waited to see what Martin would say, but he didn't say a word. Just kept sipping his coffee.

"There's something in the Manor they want," Simon said as he entered the kitchen. I almost dropped my mug. He was only half dressed. Jeans, no shirt. I didn't mean to stare, but good lord. The man was *cut*. It wasn't until Devon took the mug from me that I realized I'd been ogling Simon. Oops. Luckily, Devon grinned—and the kiss he gave me was worth making him a little jealous.

I may have ogled Simon, but Dani? She drooled.

"Dear god, man. Please put a shirt on." She laughed as she came into the kitchen.

Simon grinned and saluted her with his cup. "All for you darlin'. All for you."

I smiled because whatever game they had going on was

heating up. Amid all the chaos, some things were so basically human they couldn't be stopped.

Unless, of course, it was by a train wreck headed through my front door.

CHAPTER TWENTY-THREE

"Ladies, please. Have we not had enough drama this week? Can't a guy have breakfast in peace?" Devon asked as he tried to get the posse, consisting of my mom, Prudence, Matilda, and Hope to quiet down. I assumed Rosa and Marcy were at the café.

"You wouldn't be so smug if you'd been over to the Manor today," Prudence said.

"Why? What would I have found?" Devon asked.

"The front door wide open and a goat trampling around on the porch."

"*A goat?*"

"Yes, Pip, a goat," my mom commented.

I hadn't realized I'd said that out loud.

"You know the entire construction crew has abandoned ship!" Matilda said with a humph. "We need to get to the bottom of it."

"Oh, Marty dear, I didn't see you standing there. Good morning," Pru said.

Martin tipped his mug. "Good morning, Pru, my dear."

"Since you're here, please explain to Devon about the spiritual awakening we've witnessed," Hope said matter-of-factly. "It appears he's not aware."

"Oh, I'm aware there's been a commotion over at the house, but I have yet to see it for myself. Until then, I have to reserve judgment—which won't happen until I get some food in me."

"Of course, son, we know you need sustenance. We've got a picnic basket in the car. We'll bring it with us. Now hurry along." Matilda's tone brooked no argument.

"Is there enough for Billy?" I asked.

Devon darted a look at me, the one that said, *what are you up to?*

"And who is Billy, Pip," my mom asked.

"The goat, of course. Pun intended."

Devon burst out laughing. Dani spat out her coffee, and Simon shook his head.

"Why don't we all head over there and see what's what?" I dished up the eggs onto the plates Devon had laid out for the four of us.

"After we eat," Devon said.

The ladies all murmured something and headed out the door with Deputy O'Hara close behind Prudence. At least he had the decency to thank us for the coffee first.

Simon chuckled. "I gotta say, life around here is never dull, is it? This town reminds me of home."

"New Orleans and Luckland have something in common?" Dani asked. "Do tell."

"My aunties mostly raised me in a very tight little neighborhood. Everything was their business. And we had our share of the supernatural, believe me."

Dani studied him. "I hadn't thought of that. Maybe you do get it."

He raised his brows in response, and Devon and I shared a

look. I wondered how long it would be before they acted on their impulses.

We pulled up to the Manor not too much later, only to find the women standing on the porch in a circle, with the goat tied to the railing.

"What do you suppose they're doing?" Devon asked as we all piled out of his and Simon's rented SUV.

"Probably another game of Tarot," I answered.

"You do know it's not a card game, right?" Simon questioned.

"Very well, probably another *reading* of the Tarot."

"My Auntie Lora would have popped you upside the head for that," Simon said with a laugh.

"Does she read the cards?" Dani asked.

"Oh yeah. And palms too."

"And cooks up some amazing gumbo, as I recall," Devon said.

As we approached the house, the ground suddenly shook, the Manor's windows rattled, and a loud hiss filled the air, which oddly sounded like the furnace having a tantrum. We all stopped in our tracks, though the ladies seemed completely unperturbed.

Devon held out his hand in a stay-back motion as he cautiously crept across the lawn. I continued right behind him, my hand on his back. I noticed Simon hadn't stayed. Dani wasn't about to get left behind either.

The ladies held hands in a circle with their eyes closed, humming. The closer we got, the more I realized the ladies seemed to be doing their Founders' Day ritual. Or a séance.

Devon stopped suddenly, causing me to crash into him, and I had to stifle an *oomph.*

Matilda let go of the other women's hands and picked up a bunch of twigs, or as she called them, her cleansing tool. *Here we go.* The beginnings of a smirk pulled at Devon's lips. I wondered whether Matilda would actually burn the twigs this time. Considering she'd recently claimed she had the power to conduct a smokeless smudge, perhaps not.

Seemed that was the least of our worries though, as Deputy Martin's car came careening up the road, screeching to a stop. Martin hopped out of the car as Devon and Simon sprinted over to him. Dani and I stayed where we were and watched as Martin did a lot of hand-waving and pointing toward town. Now what had happened?

Devon and Simon raced over to their car, then with nothing more than a wave, took off behind the deputy. The women waited until the men were out of sight, then raced to their own SUV, leaving Dani and me in the front yard. No ride.

"Ideas?" Dani looked at me, hands on her hips.

"Nope. Looks as if we've been left to our own devices. Let's go in. See what the ruckus is all about."

"Let's hope it isn't really a house of cards, Pip. I didn't bring our helmets," Dani said with a chuckle. She hadn't been inside yet, or she most definitely wouldn't be laughing.

"What should we do about Billy? He seems to have a keen interest in whatever he's chewing on over there," I said.

"I think that's a scarf," Dani said.

"That can't be good for him."

I was tempted to go up and grab the scarf, but I wasn't sure I wanted to play tug-of-war. I envisioned one of Billy's hooves in my ass if I tried to yank his meal out of his mouth. Nope, not doing that. Spying a patch of loose grass, I pulled free a few handfuls, then waved them in Billy's direction, hoping it would catch Billy's eye and tempt him to drop the scarf.

Clever goat didn't bat an eye. He didn't drop the scarf either. Dani, obviously having a better idea of what goats liked, pulled a hankie from her pocket and showed Billy, who lost all interest in the scarf and headed toward her. Luckily, the rope held fast. I dashed up, grabbed the scarf, dropped the clumps of grass, and was back next to Dani in record time. Billy glared at me but eventually started munching on his healthier treat.

I checked the charcoal gray scarf and spotted a label. "Wow. Frederick Lynn. Chicago. Fancy!"

"Who around here wears custom silk scarves from Chicago?" Dani wondered.

"Now, that is an excellent question."

Dani grinned. "I'm guessing it belongs to the resident ghost."

"Let's go in and make sure everything is right as rain in there," I said. "I don't know what those women were up to, but it couldn't have been good."

I pushed open the front door, but a buzz in my pocket stopped me from going any farther.

Devon: Come to the station.

With a sigh, Dani and I said goodbye to Billy, then with the scarf in hand, headed over to the Luckland PD office—which was really just a desk and chair located at the sheriff's office.

As we stepped onto the town's main road, I caught sight of a rather large group of residents gathered out front of Devon's office. Had it been dark and had they been carrying lit torches, I would have been in the middle of a scene from Frankenstein. I could almost hear them chanting—*lock up the monster.*

CHAPTER TWENTY-FOUR

The closer we got, the louder the shouting got.

"Ghostbusters!"

"Get a priest!"

"Burn it down!"

That one was a bit shocking. *Burn what down?*

Dani and I glanced at each other. I had a terrible feeling all this was about my ramshackle estate. Mystic Manor had quite a reputation, wholly undeserved, but it seemed not only the construction crew had an aversion to ghoulish happenings, the residents of Luckland did as well.

Since when? Luckland was known for its roaming specters. Granted, it wasn't often anyone *saw* one. So, it seemed the townsfolk were fine with having the legend that brought in the tourists, but not the actual ghosts.

As we arrived, the circle of maybe twenty-five or so residents separated, clearing a little path for Dani and me to approach the sidewalk, where Deputy Martin and Devon tried to calm everyone down.

Simon stood off to the side, just observing. I looked around for the ladies, but they were nowhere to be found. I wondered about that.

"Pippa, that house of yours is a ghost factory!" yelled Tommy Thistle.

I put my hands on my hips and sighed. Tommy and I had one disastrous date in high school that I'd cut short. He'd never really forgiven me. I should have known he'd be involved with this disruption if it was directed against me and mine.

"What's got your panties in a twist now?"

"Ask Joey! Hey, Joey, tell her what happened!" Tommy shouted at the local general store delivery man. Joey looked about nervously as he tended to stutter. Everyone quietened down to help him relax.

"Joey? What happened?" I asked.

"Well. I took the paint. I mean, d-delivered the paint. For upstairs. You know?" Joey spoke slowly and deliberately, making sure he could find the right words.

"Yes, go on, please." I was careful to be patient. There was no need to make Joey suffer because Tommy was so inconsiderate.

"Well. I delivered the p-paint upstairs. I was placing it in the hall when these guys, these c-c-construction guys, ran past me. Down the stairs and out the door. All the while s-screaming. I went back downstairs. They were leaving."

Devon stepped forward. "What were they screaming? What did they say?"

"Just s-screams. Like, in the m-movies," Joey said.

"I see. When was this, Joey?" Devon asked.

"Yesterday, about five-thirty."

"And the goat?"

"What g-g-goat?" Joey asked. "No g-g-goat."

I frowned. "No goat?"

"No goat. A hunchback. Upstairs. In the w-w-window. As I was leaving."

That drew a fairly loud outburst from our Luckland street mob.

"Folks, no need to be alarmed. The deputy and I will go investigate." Devon raised both hands to quiet them down. It had no impact. "You can all head back to your homes. I'm sure we'll be able to clear this up." Devon was ever the optimist as he tried again. Unfortunately, the mob did not disperse. Then Marcy rang the bell at the Blue Sky Café across the street, which indicated fresh pies were available. That broke up the crowd, leaving just Dani, Simon, Devon, and Deputy Martin. And me, of course, still holding the silk scarf and realizing it may be more important than we understood.

Turning to Devon, I held out the scarf.

"What's this?" he asked.

"Billy's breakfast."

"I sense there's more," Devon said. "What do you have for me, Pip."

I smiled. I loved it when he asked that. "Look at the label. Expensive little number from Chicago. It wasn't in the house last time we were there, and if Billy had found it before he wandered into Mystic Manor, he would have already eaten it. Therefore, when we found him, he'd only recently picked up the scarf. So, whoever dropped it in the house is someone you might want to visit with."

"Unless they're part of the crew, Pip." Devon chewed his lip. A habit he picked up from me, no doubt. "On the other hand, if it didn't belong to one of them, there might be a stranger in our midst."

Dani chuckled. "Oh, I like that. A stranger in our midst— sounds like a made-for-Netflix movie."

"Or a dime-store detective novel." Simon snickered as he

took the scarf from Devon and placed it in a plastic sleeve he just happened to have handy.

Who kept evidence sleeves handy?

"What say we go back to the Manor and review things," Devon said. "Martin, would you mind getting a courier to come and pick up the scarf and take it to the lab in Denver?"

Deputy Martin nodded, then headed into his office muttering. "If it's not one thing, it's another. This place is a damn zoo."

The rest of us piled into the rented SUV and headed back to the Manor. When we got there, Billy was fast asleep on the porch.

I didn't know of anyone who had goats in Luckland, so I had no idea where he could have come from, but he couldn't stay out on the porch. Mystic Manor sat on a two-acre lot, most of which was untended lawn. The rear of the property was fenced in, however, so I untied the rope and gave it a tug to get Billy on his feet. Surprisingly, he was cooperative. Maybe we'd developed a kinship. I opened the wooden gate leading to the back garden and led him through. I had no idea what goats needed for sustenance, though, and as I didn't want to let him go roaming quite yet, I tied him to the fence post.

"Dani, google how to care for a goat. We probably need supplies," I said.

"Are we keeping the goat, Pip?" Devon looked at me as if I'd lost my mind.

"For now. We can't let him go roaming around by himself with no support."

"And just how do you know it's a him?"

He had me on that one. I didn't have a clue.

"Scratch that, Dani. Better call Doc Stormy." Doc was our local vet. His real name was Stanley, but he had smoldering eyes. We didn't call him Stormy to his face, of course. That would be totally inappropriate.

We put the phone on speaker when he answered.

"Hey, Doc, it's Dani Valdez. We found a goat."

"A goat? Hmm. Can't say I know anyone around with a goat. Shall I come and take a look?"

"Absolutely. The sooner, the better. We're over at the Manor," Dani said.

"The manor?" Doc asked. Clearly confused.

"Sorry, the old Tindle place."

"Ah. I see. I'll be there in a spot."

Dani chuckled as she disconnected.

"What's a spot, and why does that guy sound like Doctor Doolittle?" Simon asked.

"Just you wait, Simon. You're in for a real treat." Dani smirked, which meant she wanted to have a little fun with him. Though how he'd react was anyone's guess.

CHAPTER TWENTY-FIVE

Standing about six five in his stockinged feet, Doc Stormy looked like something out of an old western. Jeans, a flannel shirt, and a big-ass cowboy hat. If I didn't already know he was an animal doctor, I'd figure him for a bronco buster. He was not happy.

Apparently, tethering a goat was a big no-no. As if we knew. We untied Billy right away, and he started jumping up and down like a toddler. Doc approached him carefully, then, because Billy was a small goat, lifted him and held him as if he were a cat, or a puppy.

"He's a pygmy goat. I'd say about three years old. You planning on keeping him? Or did you need me to take him off your hands?" he asked while examining Billy.

I looked at Devon, who grinned. I was a sucker for animals. I wanted to keep the little guy.

"Keep him," Devon said. His grin widened even as he shook his head.

"Then you ought to know he'll need a companion. They

aren't meant to live the single life. Goats are herd animals. I'll find you a mate."

"You're a goat matchmaker?" Dani asked, chuckling.

I knew what was coming. The guys didn't know Dani and I had some history with Doc. We'd gone out with him at one time or another, primarily out of curiosity. He was polite, chivalrous even, but dull as a cork.

"I match humans too." He directed his attention toward Dani. "How about dinner tonight?"

I looked at Simon, just to see how he'd react. He scowled and crossed his arms over his chest.

Dani smirked.

"We've got plans." Simon stepped forward and held out his hand. "Simon Boudreaux. We haven't met."

"Stanley Stormburger, DVM," Doc replied.

I assumed he waited for Simon to indicate not just who he was but what he was. When Simon simply stared, Doc cleared his throat.

"Moving on, you'll need a shelter and hay rack for him. And his new girlfriend. I have just the one. I'll bring her around tomorrow. The fencing is a good height, at least five feet, so he won't get out. In the meantime, there's a shed back there that old man Tindle built. With a few modifications, it'll work just fine. Luckland Mercantile has got some good straw feed down at the store. Have Joey bring out a few bales. And make sure you've got a bucket of water in there as well. Any questions?"

Doc looked around. I had a million questions, but he didn't appear to be in the mood to answer them. We all watched as he carefully set Billy down and closed the gate. With a tip of his hat, Doc left.

I crouched and peered at Billy through the gap in the wooden posts. "Hey, bud. Looks as if you're gonna be around for a while. Keep an eye on things, would you?" I spoke softly as he watched me. "If you promise to be good, I'll get you a new scarf too."

I would have sworn by all that was holy that goat jumped up and did a little jig. I didn't know whether to laugh or be terrified.

Devon's phone went off as I stood, and he and Simon walked about ten yards away. I was fairly certain the call was related to the dearly departed soul on the Mullet Madness bus.

"Say, Pip, did you hear something?" Dani whispered suddenly, her expression full of concentration.

"No," I replied, but held my breath and waited.

"That, there." Dani grabbed my hand, and I nodded. I did hear something that time. A clanking came from inside the house. Or underneath. As if someone was banging on the pipes.

It was rhythmic and deliberate. We stood there, frozen. Even Billy had perked up his ears. Simon and Devon strolled back. No, not strolled. They strode briskly. All business. I quickly held up a hand before they could speak and put a finger to my lips, gesturing toward the house. They exchanged a worried look and stopped to listen. I could tell they were just as concerned as Dani and me. Simon nodded toward the street, pointing at us. I think he tried to indicate Dani and I should leave and let them handle it. As if.

When they pulled out their guns, I did reconsider, just not enough to move.

They crept up the stairs, then each stood on either side of the open doorway, backs against the wall, operating as one. They nodded at each other, then turned and went inside at the same time, like in a scene from CSI.

Dani and I sat on the porch and waited.

"Where do you think the posse has run off to?" Dani asked.

"I guess they're either plotting something, or they've gone

off investigating." The latter option worried me. Whatever happened down in Tucson was *not* for amateurs.

"I don't want to get left behind," Dani muttered. "I'm never here for the good stuff."

"I'm always here, and I still get left behind." I chuckled even though it wasn't funny.

"Stop griping, girls," Devon said from behind us, making us jump like beans.

"Easy for you to say, Dev. You're always in the thick of it."

"Well, the house is clear. No ghosts or humans. So, let's go home."

"In a minute." I had to take care of Billy, so I quickly called the mercantile to order food and supplies. Then I called my dad, as there was no way my practically perfect boyfriend had an ounce of handyman in him. If he did, I'd never seen it. The shed out back was a bit dilapidated last time I checked, and someone needed to shore it up before I'd feel comfortable with our new pet lounging in it. I couldn't have the ceiling caving in on him.

Devon took a seat next to me, stretching his legs down the porch steps as Simon leaned against the railing by Dani.

"You guys don't really think Trey Marks killed that guy, do you?" Though it was an odd time to throw that question out there, we'd avoided the subject for hours now, and I couldn't rein in my impatience any longer.

"Can't really talk about it, Pip. Sorry." Devon patted my leg. As if that would help.

"Why not?" Dani demanded.

"Because it's an ongoing investigation," Simon said. "However, I have a theory I can share regarding those threatening phone calls the ladies received when someone said they knew the ladies' secrets. What if one of the secrets was knowing Matilda had an illegitimate child? Devon, what if that threat was to tell Trey about you and to tell you that you were Matilda's son, not her nephew?"

"It's too late for me, I already know, but you might be on to something regarding Trey. Matilda swore he was in that bus, so maybe the dead guy was in there to tell Trey about me. We need to convene a meeting of the posse. Tonight. Pip, gather the troops. We'll all meet at my mom's at seven."

Devon had a habit of expecting things. He tended to blur the lines between his professional and personal life to the point where some people automatically obeyed. I might have argued with him, but I was too damn curious about what he and Simon were thinking.

"Just remember, as far as the posse are concerned, you don't know about any threats, so you'll have to figure a way of broaching the subject before discussing Trey." I looked from Devon to Simon, hoping they cooperated. Even so, it was past time to find out what those secrets were.

I waved the boys off as my dad arrived. Dani and I decided to help him create a comfortable abode for Billy. I had grown so attached to the little goat I wondered if 99 might get jealous. I hoped they'd get along. I'd already gathered some information from the internet, and it seemed cats and goats generally did get along. It was a wait and see kind of thing though.

By the time my dad had fortified the shed, and we'd filled it with straw and a wonderful blanket for Billy to cozy up on, I was determined he and 99 would be lifelong friends. Hopefully, they would see it the same way.

After my dad left, Dani and I made the short walk home and discovered the boys already out back, manning the grill—which meant with a beer in one hand, spatula in another, and playing verbal one-upmanship while going down memory lane. Not ones to look a gift horse in the mouth, Dani and I grabbed drinks and got comfy on the back porch to watch the guys work.

It was a very domestic scene all in all. Maybe too domestic for Dani as she suddenly started tapping her leg nervously. I knew that tap. I grabbed her hand, pulling her up with me to distract her.

"Come on, Dani girl, let's set the table." It was time for us to have a little talk. Not something the boys needed to hear.

CHAPTER TWENTY-SIX

"No. Absolutely not. We are *not* having a séance at the Manor tonight." Devon gritted his teeth and put his phone on speaker while Matilda continued to prattle.

"But, Devon, dear boy, it's the only way. Trust your mother on this."

"Not happening. Nope. Not now, not ever," he said through his clenched jaw.

We'd just finished eating a somewhat late lunch when his phone had gone off. At first, the phone call seemed normal. It was only when his eyes started to go wide and his nose flared I realized we were in for an interesting conversation.

He placed the phone on the counter and began pacing around the kitchen.

"The moon is full. It will amplify our abilities," Matilda declared. "With you there, it will have synergy."

"Mom, as much as I love you, this is nuts."

I wondered why he was being so argumentative. If our visions of ghosts were anything to go by, he'd shown some strong intuitive powers or psychic energy like me.

"Devon, what if we agreed to meet up at the Manor but not call it a séance," I said. "Would that be preferable?"

He raised his brows at me.

"Fine. We'll meet up with you. But no séance." Devon sighed, knowing it was hopeless. "We'll see you in a bit." Disconnecting, he shook his head. "Pip, how can you encourage them?" He was miffed, apparently.

"Because there's an awful lot going on, and if a harmless little psychic experience can clear it up, let's give it a go." There was no point in denying I'd begun to believe in all the hocus-pocus like Tarot cards and psychic readings. How could I not after everything that had happened? "Think about it, boy genius. Maybe our ghostly miner will make an appearance."

***

We arrived to find the women on the porch, peering in the windows. I knew they had a key, so I wondered what kept them outside. They were all dressed in black once more—apart from the colorful scarves around their necks. I speculated whether they were from the same shop as the one Billy had snacked on earlier. Looking back, maybe I should have given it more thought, though I couldn't figure why they'd wear scarves from a men's haberdashery.

Devon strode briskly up the steps, forcing the women to move aside to let him through. He really was quite grumpy about the whole séance thing.

We all filed in once Devon unlocked the door. With the disappearance of the reno crew, the place was eerily empty. The main staircase wore the tattered remains of a red carpet. To the left was the set of French doors leading into the infamous parlor—the one where the previous tenants had held us hostage. The room could be potentially fabulous once I'd erased all memory of having a gun pointed at my head. The parlor stretched from the front to the back of the house, with large rectangular windows that lined the front and side wall. Eventually, the room would be our conservatory, but right now, it seemed to be the ladies' choice for their gathering. With the moonlight shining brightly into the room, it certainly had the vibe.

My mom led the way, carrying her *bag of fun,* as we liked to call the enormous tote bag that held all kinds of surprises. She always said it was best to be prepared. I always wondered what the hell she prepared for. She reached in and pulled out a wadded-up bundle, untied it, then shook it out to unveil an enormous midnight blue bed sheet covered in stars, which she laid on the floor.

"Sit, sit!" Matilda said, clapping her hands. Usually, my mother was the hand clapper, but I supposed this was a special occasion.

"Wait," I said. "Where's Babs?"

"Couldn't make it, something about watching paint dry."

"Why doesn't that surprise me," I muttered.

"She was doing a few touch-ups," my mom said as she patted me on the shoulder. "Seems Leah found the Sharpies and decided to do a mural."

"Well, I hope Babs took a picture before covering it up. She can use that later to keep Leah in line." Prudence grinned as she stepped into the center of the sheet and placed a bowl on the floor. It looked like potpourri but smelled like garlic.

"Are we expecting blood-suckers?" Simon asked. It seemed as if he decided that would be a good conversation starter.

"My dear boy, sit yourself down and behave," Rosa retorted as she grabbed his hand to pull him down on one side of her while Dani sat on the other.

I landed between Prudence and Marcy, while Devon ended up between Hope and my mother.

"Sorry to be late! Did I miss anything?" My dad rushed in and took a seat between Simon and Matilda.

Though surprised to see him, maybe I shouldn't have been. I grinned. "As there are currently no hovering spirits to be seen, clearly not, Dad."

"Good, good." He rubbed his hands together. "I've got some questions, so hopefully, this is more successful than last time."

"Last time?" Devon looked at my dad. "You do this often?"

"Oops." My dad's expression turned sheepish, and I wondered why he wanted to talk to someone from the other side. And who.

Without a word, Matilda took Simon and my dad's hands in hers and nodded for all of us to link hands as well. First thing I noticed was Prudence's cold hands, but Marcy's were hot. Seriously hot. Not sweaty, more like hot coals. I darted a glance at her, and she just smiled. Perhaps she was channeling the Native Americans' magic that saturated the land on which Luckland was built, which was supposed to increase the ladies' natural abilities.

Matilda began chanting in a low voice. I had to strain to hear her.

"Good spirits of the moon, the stars, and the universe at large, welcome. We ask for your sage guidance and wisdom, so we understand our mission. We humbly beseech you to join us and guide us in our journey. Let us begin."

"Kate?" Matilda looked to her right and nodded.

My mom closed her eyes, took a breath, and opened them again. "Good spirits, I ask you to guide us on our mission and humbly beseech you to answer this question." She raised her hands, along with Devon's and Matilda's.

"Someone is attempting to keep what is ours. Who?"

I assumed she meant who had the six shoeboxes that had gone missing at the beginning of spring. We all waited for something to happen, but nothing did. Kate lowered her hands and turned to Devon, nodding. He tipped his head and looked at her questioningly.

"Your turn. Ask whatever you like," she whispered to him.

So, being the good guy, he raised his hands, including Hope's and my mom's, closed his eyes, took a breath, and opened them. I could tell he was trying not to laugh.

"Good spirits, I ask you to guide us on our mission and humbly beseech you to answer this question." He turned to Kate. I assumed to confirm he said it correctly. "When will Pippa say yes?"

I glared at him. He hadn't asked me to do anything that required a yes. He grinned like a hyena. I turned red as a beet. Again, thankfully, nothing happened.

Meanwhile, all the women snickered. The men too. Always at my expense, of course.

It was Hope's turn next.

"Should we buy the bakery?" Hope asked. I had no idea they were contemplating buying out their only competition in town. The bakery, attached to the Luckland Inn, wasn't a full café, but it did take a bite out of the morning market.

A sudden breeze blew by. All the windows had been closed before we started. Now, a distinct coffee aroma, strong enough to mask the garlic, filled the room. I gasped softly and looked to see if anyone else noticed. Dani, Simon, and Devon all looked startled. The others, not so much.

The women simply smiled. Hope put her hands down, and Marcy raised hers. Rinse and repeat. Marcy asked if they needed to create more recipes, but there was no response. Then it was my turn. I had a zillion questions to ask, but I knew better than to ask the one to which I needed an answer.

"Pass," I said.

Everyone looked at me. Matilda shook her head. "No, dear, you must ask."

"Fine." I looked at Devon and tipped my head. "Good spirits, I ask you to guide us on our mission and humbly beseech you to answer this question."

Devon grinned.

"Is Devon hiding secrets from me?" I asked the dear, sweet spirit guides.

Devon's smile disappeared as his eyes widened.

The ground shook. Seriously shook. The windows rattled, and the light fixture above us swung from side to side.

"You all felt that, right?" I asked immediately. Looking around, I knew they did. Holy moly.

"Relax, Pip, it was an earthquake," Devon said. "A small one. Three point nine." He chewed on his lip, a sign of his nervousness.

I smirked. "As opposed to what, a two point five? You have a seismometer in your pocket?"

Matilda jumped to the rescue. "Pru, your turn."

While I worried about what Devon hid from me, everyone else focused on Prudence, who wanted to know whether this thing with Marty would last. She and the deputy had been high school sweethearts, finally given a second chance. Seemed the spirits were in her favor as she got a text message from him right at that moment.

Dani asked about her next job, her mom asked how many grandchildren Dani and Simon would give her, and Simon asked if he was dreaming. My dad asked if he'd ever learn to keep a secret, causing the group to burst into laughter. Then it was Matilda's turn. Suddenly, everyone went still. This show was hers, after all.

"Will I find him?" That was all she said. Barely audible.

Tears filled my eyes because she wanted to know about Trey, her long-lost love. I hoped she'd get a sign. I kind of expected one, but the Native American lady who appeared directly behind Matilda had me thinking I was seeing things. Yes, I'd seen the man at the barn and the dwarf miner in the woods, but nothing prepared me for the tall, beautiful woman dressed in what I assumed was traditional garb with brightly colored beads sewn into her tunic and threaded through her long, silky hair. She slowly gazed around the circle, her dark eyes locking on each of us before she placed her hand on Matilda's shoulder.

Matilda jerked, and her eyes widened. "What's behind me?" she whispered.

My mom, Prudence, and Hope closed their eyes and started muttering something that sounded like their annual Founders' Day ritual. I didn't know the exact words because I didn't pay much attention when they stood in their circle and promised not to disturb the sacred burial grounds on which Luckland was allegedly built. In return for us not digging up their bones, the spirits were apparently not supposed to rise and murder everyone. Or something like that.

A high keening drowned out the ladies' muttering then a bright light filled the room. I squinted. Then the light suddenly disappeared, the keening stopped, and the ladies all sucked in a deep breath.

The residual silence in the room was deafening—until the crunch and screech of metal on metal outside broke it.

CHAPTER TWENTY-SEVEN

Devon jumped up and took off with Simon close behind, yelling at the rest of us to stay put. As if. We waited maybe thirty seconds before zipping out after them, though we remained on the porch at the sight of the twisted heap of metal that had crashed into the big oak tree in the front yard.

"Is anyone hurt?"

"Are they dead?"

"Whose car is that?"

I tuned out the women's questions, but Dani and I glanced at each other as though we had similar thoughts. As far as I could tell, there was no mangled body. No blood. Not even a smoky engine. On TV, whenever a car crashed into a tree, smoke and bloody bodies usually ensued. There should at least be a driver.

A few minutes later, Deputy Martin drove up, sirens blaring. A few minutes after that, he departed. As I realized nobody was going to be loaded into either a meat wagon or a hearse, I cautiously approached.

"Pip, a little privacy. This is police work," Devon said.

"My front lawn has the makings of a junkyard. That's not

private," I said in a huff. "Furthermore, where's the driver? How could anyone walk, or run, away from this so fast you didn't catch them?"

The way Devon and Simon looked at each other, something was up.

"Don't tell me you think a ghost drove the car." I was prepared to believe a lot of things after what I'd just witnessed, but a ghostly Evel Knievel was not one of them. "Either the car *had* no driver, or they got away, and I don't believe you'd let someone who smashed into our yard get away. So, what's going on?"

The boys ignored me and stepped into a private huddle. I sighed in frustration and turned to stomp back up onto the porch. After a brief conversation where no one mentioned the séance and the vision it created, the women piled into their vehicle while my dad climbed into his. Dani stayed behind with me to wait. I was too hyped up and curious to leave. With so much happening, it was enough just to focus my attention on one crisis, let alone multiple disasters. My hanging around for answers ended up all for nothing though. The local mechanic towed away the car, and the guys suggested we all head back home, promising to update us when we got there.

The moment we headed inside my rented cottage, I brought out a bottle of wine and four glasses. Simon broke out a bottle of scotch and a couple of tumblers.

"What's wrong with a good vino, Simon?" I asked.

"Scotch is a man's drink," he replied with a grin.

"I wasn't aware that alcohol had Y chromosomes," Dani commented, giving him a sidelong glance. I eyed the two of them as they eyed each other.

"Listen, we need to talk about what's going on over at the Manor—other than what happened at the séance." Devon leaned on the fireplace mantel and swirled his scotch. I didn't know whether he deliberately tried to be the sexy male detective, or he did so subconsciously.

"So, you did see the Native American?" I asked, just wanting to clarify. I couldn't tell if he'd seen her, though he had gone a little pale.

Devon reluctantly nodded.

"I saw her too," Dani said. She stared at Simon, who also nodded.

"How about we ignore our phantom visitor for now and figure out who crashed into our tree and why," Devon said.

"According to the papers in the glove compartment, Hunter Jackson rented the car," Simon remarked. "From what Pippa told Devon, and my subsequent research, Hunter is too skilled a driver to crash accidentally. So, we think he deliberately drove his car into the tree. When we tried to contact him, he didn't answer his phone, and he wasn't at home when Martin went to check."

"Did you check Morgan's house?" I asked. "Remember, she's smitten with him."

Devon nodded. "Yes, I also got Martin to check there. She wasn't at home either."

I frowned. "Okay, but what's Hunter's reason? There isn't one, unless... Oh, what if he's trying to keep people away from the house? He crashed his car to get us out. What if he got the crew to leave by setting up a rig or something and made them think they saw and heard ghosts?"

Dani snorted. "After what we've just witnessed, they probably did see and hear ghosts, but I agree, it seems he wanted the house to remain empty."

"What's his aim? Why does he want no one at the house?" Simon asked.

"The gold," Dani said. "He's probably figured the map at the town hall isn't real, but I bet he thinks the gold is beneath the

Manor. Morgan probably told him the ladies own it and are descendants of our illustrious founders. He also may have seen them trying to dig up the yard and assumed they were also looking for the gold."

"Good point," Devon said quietly. "Simon contacted the map store owner in Denver and found out Morgan went in and asked about star navigational maps, so we know they're interested in the gold. But why did Hunter come to Luckland now? It seems as if the gold has become the focus of attention for a lot of people recently. Ever since the shoeboxes went missing."

"So, do we all now believe a gold vein exists in Luckland, and information about it is in the shoeboxes? We know a copy of the original founders' map is in there. And, talking about maps..." I set my focus on Devon. "Are you going to admit you took the one behind the picture from your mother's house?"

"Wouldn't it be better in a safe place and not where anyone could find it?"

That wasn't really an answer, but reading between the lines, I could reasonably guess he'd hidden it somewhere. Maybe because he knew I wasn't any good at keeping secrets, he thought it would be best not to admit anything. I could have been annoyed, I *should* be, but when it came down to it, I trusted him.

"The gold isn't our only worry though. What's more troubling is the *other* secrets in those boxes." That was our worst nightmare. Someone had possession of all the ladies' secrets. "If we can't find the boxes, then maybe we could organize some damage control before the damage happens. We need to force the posse's hand."

I texted my mom, Devon texted his, and Dani texted hers. Then we waited. We all got the same response.

It isn't time.

Well, that was helpful.

"Devon, you need to go over and explain to your mother the seriousness of our situation."

"You'll have to explain it to your mother as well."

"What about me?" Dani queried.

"I'll take care of your mother, Dani. She likes me." Simon seemed awfully smug about it.

I shook my head. "Has anyone forgotten that they're all together? It'll be one for all and all for one."

We got back in the car and headed over to Matilda's, where we assumed they were. We were wrong, and it was clear from the lack of lights in any of their houses that were literally next door to each other they weren't home—which could mean only one thing.

"The cabin!" Devon and I said in unison.

CHAPTER TWENTY-EIGHT

The cabin was a good forty-minute drive up the mountains and was where the ladies went when they didn't wish anyone to disturb them. Not that it would stop us. Last time we were up there, Prudence had run away. I couldn't blame her. She thought aliens were harassing her. Turned out it was just a really nasty case of a stalking ex, who ironically turned out to be a gold-digging hypnotist.

We headed up the long drive lined with low-emission solar lamps to what was more of a magnificently designed luxury home than a cabin. My little cottage could fit on the cabin's front porch.

The ladies must have seen us coming because all the lights immediately went out. Undeterred, we hopped out of the car and marched up the steps where Devon did what I called the police rap on the door. Very brusque and emphatic knocks.

When the women didn't respond, he tried the door handle. Locked. He called them. No answer. As Devon continued to knock, he motioned to Simon to head around the back. As if that would work.

Simon returned, shaking his head in defeat.

"Use your key," I said to Devon.

He turned to me and frowned. "What key?"

"You don't have a key?" With a grin, I searched through my keyring and triumphantly held up a key to the cabin.

"Where did you get that?" Devon asked.

"I thought it prudent we carry a spare, so when my dad wasn't looking, I grabbed his key and got one made."

He grinned from ear to ear and leaned down to give me a kiss. It seemed he'd learned to appreciate me. About time—it had only taken our entire lives.

I unlocked the door, and we tiptoed in.

It was quiet inside. The women were hiding somewhere, and while the cabin was massive, it was quite open on the main floor with one large, great room with soaring ceilings. No real hiding opportunities. They had to be upstairs, probably in a closet somewhere. Even the closets were massive, so they could all fit inside one. But which closet and were they all together or hiding separately? Knowing the women, as we checked one place, they'd migrate to another. I could already picture them holding hands and sneaking from room to room.

"I say we split up," I whispered. "We can cover the four main rooms on the west side, then hit the guest suites on the other end."

"How about you girls stay here, and Simon and I will search upstairs," Devon said quietly.

"Not gonna happen, super sleuth." I crossed my arms over my chest for emphasis, making Dani compress her lips, trying not to laugh. It was hard to act naturally and respond appropriately when we had to be silent as mice.

Devon and Simon stealthily crept upstairs with Dani and me close behind. A sudden thud from my mom's room gave the ladies away. They weren't in the main room, so Devon opened the closet door and found all the women looking incredibly ticked off—which was fine because I didn't particularly like having to play hide and seek either.

Devon shook his head. "Ladies, I'm going to suggest we all head downstairs. We need to talk."

They followed us downstairs but immediately went into ladies' auxiliary mode, where they pretended we were having a routine gathering and not an intervention. Hope and Marcy headed to the kitchen to prepare a feast while my mother and Prudence hit the wet bar to set up drinks. Matilda and Rosa discussed what to watch on the big screen TV as if nothing out of the ordinary were taking place. As if they hadn't found a dead body. As if a car hadn't crashed into a tree outside Mystic Manor. As if the séance had never happened and a ghost hadn't appeared. As if everything were completely normal.

Devon didn't even bother to try and hide his impatience. He strode over to the fireplace and rested his elbow on the mantle, tapping his fingers. Once everyone had settled in the living room, he began to pace.

"All right. We need to resolve a few things here and now. Namely, just what the hell is in those shoeboxes? Aside from a copy of the map you kept on the wall. I suspect, and correct me if I'm wrong, those shoeboxes contain all kinds of secrets you women have been hiding for years. How am I doing so far?"

"We've been over this, Devon. The boxes contain confidential information we aren't at liberty to discuss," Matilda said.

"I see. You realize whoever has them might use that information against you. Do you not think it would be wise to find out who? Maybe stop them?"

"Against us? Whatever do you mean?" Matilda asked.

"Mom, I was an FBI agent, and now I'm a cop. Surely you must know I'd figure out someone was threatening you all with the secrets in those boxes."

The glares the ladies gave me should have made me cringe,

but Devon hadn't admitted I'd told him about the threats, and for that, I loved him even more. I shrugged in a *don't look at me* kind of way.

"Well, you're right, Dev, but we're quite confident it was the Panellos who threatened us, and they're in jail. I doubt they could hurt us from in there, so there is nothing for us to worry about," Matilda said.

"The Panellos admitted they never opened the boxes. They handed off the four they bought to a couple they met. So, someone else has those boxes. Someone else also has one or both of the other two boxes."

The ladies all looked stricken, and every single one of them started talking at once.

"Ladies. Ladies!" Devon waved his arms, but no one took any notice.

I whistled shrilly to shut them up. Worked every time.

"Thank you," Devon said.

I smiled in acknowledgment.

Hope cleared her throat. "Okay. So, if it wasn't the Panellos, then someone else must have discovered our most personal information. Things we kept tucked away. For ourselves," she announced. "They must be the ones who want to hurt us."

"We've established that, Hope. What information?" Devon asked.

"Well, we don't know what information. We don't know which box or boxes they have. You said it yourself, Devon. Several people may have the boxes. So, if we don't know what box they have, then we don't know what secret they have." Hope said all that as if it made sense, which it kind of did. "The calls we received during book club were not specific."

Devon quickly glanced at me. "Phone calls? Book club?"

Bless him. He was still pretending I hadn't told him anything.

Hope nodded. "Yes. We each received a call, and the person at the other end of the phone said they knew our secrets."

"That's it? They knew your secrets? Did they demand money? Have you received additional calls?" Simon asked.

"No, we haven't heard a peep since then," Prudence said.

"Which may not be a good thing. They could be gearing up to expose everything they know. Now, if you would just tell us what's in *all* the boxes, we can minimize any possible embarrassment," Devon said.

Though I was sure they had several secrets, I doubted anything could top their secret of stumbling upon a bag of stolen millions in Vegas and keeping it. I waited to hear what they would say.

When no one said anything else, Devon sighed in frustration. "I understand your concerns in not revealing your secrets, but a man died in that bus in Tucson, which might relate to what's in those boxes."

"How? There could be no conceivable connection between that dead man and us," my mom said.

Devon turned to Matilda. "What about Trey? If you heard him in that bus before you found the body, as you claim, then there *is* a connection between you. Was one of the secrets in the boxes about Trey being my father?"

After a few seconds of silence, Marcy spoke. "We may have to fess up, girls. The cards were quite clear."

Devon raised an eyebrow. "Anything you'd like to share?"

The women all looked at one another, which took a while since they sat scattered about the different sofas. Finally, they seemed to reach a consensus because Matilda sighed.

"I may have found something," she whispered.

CHAPTER TWENTY-NINE

Curiosity had me at the edge of my seat, and I barely constrained myself from demanding Matilda tell us, but this was Devon's show.

"What did you find?" Devon asked.

"A photo."

"I can't help if I don't have the details," he said gently.

"A photo of Trey and me when we met."

"Where did you find it?"

"That man had it. The dead one." She sat a bit taller. Building up her defenses, it seemed. "I took it back."

"You stole evidence from a dead body, and you're only telling us now?" Simon asked, shocked.

"Yes."

Devon took a deep breath, then exhaled slowly. "Can I assume the photo was in one of the boxes?"

When Matilda nodded, Devon sighed. So, there *was* a connection between the women and the dead man, and it seemed the man may have had one of the ladies' boxes.

"Say, look at that!" Prudence suddenly pointed the remote at the TV and turned up the volume. On the screen was a mugshot of what appeared to be a very angry man. The disembodied voiceover explained that Tony the Tiger was found dead in an RV park in Tucson. I had no idea who Tony the Tiger was, but I was pretty sure he was our tour bus buddy. Or body.

The voice continued to explain that Tony the Tiger had recently been released from prison, having served seven years for armed robbery and extortion.

"He might have been trying to extort money from Trey, but I can't see how an old photo of Trey and Matilda would necessarily be a secret or worth anything. Was there other evidence in the box that Trey was Devon's father?" I asked.

"A copy of Devon's birth certificate," Matilda said.

"So, Tony must have figured Trey didn't know about Devon and was trying to get Trey to pay up to keep quiet," I said. "Except, wouldn't Tony have been better trying to get money off you, Matilda?"

"Who knows what goes on in the minds of criminals," said my mom. "The man was nothing but an evil opportunist."

I could have said the same about the ladies and their stolen millions, but I kept my mouth shut.

Dani frowned. "How could Trey have killed Tony? I mean, Trey's over sixty, and Tony doesn't seem like an easy pushover."

Devon winced, and I could tell he hadn't wanted to accept his father could kill anyone, but the evidence seemed to be mounting.

"Trey's a blackbelt," Matilda said, her tone miserable.

I winced then. Things were not looking good for Trey Marks.

The front door suddenly flew open, and we all jumped. My stomach lodged in my throat until I realized who it was.

"Jesus, Babs, can't you at least knock?"

"Can't you at least include me? Why am I the last to know about a horrific car crash at the Manor? I thought it was you."

"How did you know we were all up here?"

"Martin O'Hara stopped by, looking for Pru. He said he checked all the ladies' houses, and everyone had disappeared. I may not be the sharpest pitchfork in the barn, but this was an easy one."

That was when I realized Tom was right behind her with Leah in tow. "You figured out they were all up here?"

"No, silly, I called Dad, who figured out they were all up here."

"Well, we aren't going to get anywhere tonight talking in circles, but I want you ladies to really think about telling the truth. No more secrets and lies. I need to know what someone has on you, and I need to find out who they are before they reveal something seriously damaging." Devon came over and helped me up. "I think we should all get some rest. We'll reconvene in the morning."

"But we just got here," Babs whined.

"Quite sensible, Devon." Matilda began waving her finger around. "You boys take one guest room and you girls the other. I'll bunk with Kate. Babs, Tom, and Leah, you can have my suite."

That pacified Babs.

Simon and Devon gave each other that look they got when they were about to do something. Together. I, for one, was determined to accompany them wherever they were going. So, the minute they started inching toward the door, I went over and placed my arm around Devon's, smiling sweetly.

"And where might we be headed, Devon dear," I asked.

"Phone call?"

"Try again." I was not going to be left behind.

Ultimately, Dani and I ended up back in the boy's SUV, headed home. I tried to give them privacy, allowing them to discuss their "official business," but sometimes it was hard to stay out of things. Like when Devon wondered aloud why Trey's background never mentioned a black belt. Or any belt, for that matter.

"You know guys do lie about that stuff," Dani said.

"You're accusing my father of lying to my mother?" Devon looked into the rearview mirror to glare at her.

That was better than Trey actually having the skills to bump off someone.

"No, Devon, I'm accusing a lounge lizard of stretching the truth to hook up with a hot chick thirty years ago," Dani retorted.

I burst out laughing. Even Simon couldn't help but grin. Eventually, one side of Devon's mouth curled up, and I knew we had him.

By the time we got home, it was well after midnight. Dani and I headed upstairs to bed, leaving Simon and Devon alone to figure things out.

CHAPTER THIRTY

Waking up to the smell of warm donuts was my favorite kind of wake-up call, especially if the aroma mingled with coffee. I'd barely run a comb through my curls before bounding downstairs. I sat at the kitchen counter, restlessly waiting while Devon brought my coffee and donut to me. After satisfying myself with an enormous bite of goodness, I turned to him.

"Well? What puzzles have you solved, Inspector?"

"We've solved the mystery of the unknown driver."

I dropped my donut. "Who? It *was* Hunter, wasn't it."

"Patience, Pip."

"Did you arrest him? Is he behind bars? Was Morgan part of it?" I had tons of questions.

"You better put your coffee down for a moment." He grinned. I did as instructed and continued waiting, impatient.

"Well?" At least a minute had passed.

"It would be rude not to wait for Dani," Simon said as he entered the kitchen.

"You two are quite mean. If I knew, I'd tell."

"Because you don't know how to keep a secret," Devon said. As if I didn't know that.

I drummed my fingers on the table, then decided to take matters into my own hands. I flew up the stairs, calling for Dani to get her ass out of bed, then raced back down, hoping to catch the boys in conversation. Instead, I found them leaning against the counter, side by side, legs crossed, mugs in hand, looking a bit too smug.

Thankfully, Dani was quick to join us, complete with bedhead. I had to give it to her. Most women would have hesitated before facing the likes of Simon with even so much as a hair out of place, myself included. I envied her self-confidence.

"Okay, I'm here. Where's the fire?" she asked while holding out her hand, presumably expecting someone to hand her coffee.

Simon did the honors, pouring her a mug as he raised an eyebrow and smirked at her disheveled appearance. She sat with me at the table, and we signaled we were ready for the bombshell.

"Our invisible stunt driver was, indeed, Hunter." Devon paused to let it sink in. "With help from his apparently bungling assistant, Morgan."

"Are they in jail? It's a crime, you know, crashing into our tree like that." Even though I'd suspected they were the culprits, I was disappointed Morgan would be involved in something like that.

"According to their statements, they were hired by the BMC Film Institute. Paid to stage the scene as a freelance project."

Whoa. Kind of a nutty explanation. "That seems pretty far-fetched, Dev. I mean, where was the film crew? The cameras? The sound engineer?"

Dani nodded. "Exactly my thinking. I've been on film shoots when diving. It's industry standard to have a lot of people around with equipment, you know, filming?" She was blatantly more sarcastic than me.

"Seems Morgan was filming it all from a distance," Simon explained. "She used her phone to capture all the action, then emailed the footage to the film company. All very legit, they claim. They also claim they were the ones who caused all the mystical mayhem at the Manor. Again, filming it."

"Wait, they're claiming they *created* the earthquake, the apparitions?" I shook my head. "No way was the Native American woman a fake. We all saw her."

Simon shrugged. "I'm only stating what they claim."

"It *could* have been a fake, Pip," Dani said. "Hologram projectors are easy to obtain."

"And the earthquake?"

"I'm sure when we question them further, they'll have a good explanation," Devon said.

I didn't believe it was all a sham, but I had no proof it was real. "Then why didn't Hunter tell everyone it was fake? The whole construction crew left."

"Precisely my thinking, Pip. Hunter and Morgan *claim* they couldn't say anything, or they wouldn't get those fabulous Frankenstein mob shots in front of my office," Devon said.

Simon chuckled. "Sounds as if they were hired for some sort of staged fictional reality show."

"Sounds as if they're full of goat turds," I grumbled. "I still think they're after the gold and believe it's beneath the Manor. Did you give them a lie detector test? And what about the scarf? Was it Hunter's?"

"No to the lie detector, but yes to the scarf. Martin asked Hunter about it, who admitted it was his. He said he must have dropped it when he'd gone into the Manor to set up the 'hauntings.' So, they've been released on their own recognizance," Devon said. Suddenly he furrowed his brows and stared at his phone.

"What is it?" I asked.

"Seems they've located Trey," he said quietly. "We have to go."

He and Simon were out the door before Dani and I could respond.

Not more than a couple of minutes later, the incessant foghorn of the Luxmobile blared right outside. Dani and I headed out to find my mom hanging out the window of the monster RV, which Prudence had parked with the engine still running.

"Girls, we're off. Back in a few days. Mind the fort!" She pulled her head back in, slid the window shut, and they were gone.

"What just happened?" I asked as we sat at the kitchen bench.

"Maybe they also know where Trey is," Dani said.

"Which would mean they're going wherever Devon and Simon went."

Dani unlocked her phone, scrolled a bit, and looked up.

"Mullet Madness. Heartland Events Center. Nebraska."

"Yeah, but Trey wouldn't be *there*. I mean, he's a fugitive, right?" I didn't think anyone could be that dumb.

Dani smirked. "Hide in plain sight, they always say."

"Then we're going too." I grabbed my phone and fired off a text to Devon.

Me: Luxmobile in motion. Come get us. We're going with you.

Devon: Where are they headed?

I didn't answer him. If I kept him hanging, he'd come back for us, which he did.

CHAPTER THIRTY-ONE

"WHAT KIND OF FLYING MACHINE IS THIS?" I THOUGHT MY QUESTION perfectly legit, considering I stood in front of one of those little puddle jumpers that sat eight tiny humans and had propellers instead of jet engines.

"It's a commuter flight," Devon commented.

"No, a commuter flight is usually a commuter jet. This is not. This is a toy airplane."

"Best we could do under short notice," Simon said with a chuckle.

I didn't have a fear of flying, really. What I had was a fear of tiny little prop planes flown by some fresh-faced kid with a Red Bull in his hand and a plastic set of wings pinned to a brand-new white collared shirt.

Okay, I could handle the short trip to Nebraska. I'd be fine, and I repeated the mantra as I climbed the rickety stairs to the plane. I ducked and turned toward the seats, then stopped in my tracks. There were eight seats in total—four rows, one seat on each side. I looked at Devon in horror. Four of the seats already had passengers. It wasn't pretty.

"Oh my god, they're clowns," Dani whispered behind me as

she bumped into my back. My fault for stopping so suddenly. I'd forgotten it was Halloween. We were on our way to the Mullet Madness Halloween Spooktacular. I had no idea where these four clowns were headed, but right about then, I considered bailing because if they were going where we were going, this would be a very long trip.

They all smiled and said hello. I think they smiled. I couldn't tell. They had smiles painted on. Never a good look. Made their teeth look yellow. At least they occupied the back four seats, so I didn't have to look at them the whole way. My imagination, however, got the best of me. Once we were seated, I leaned close to Devon.

"If the fuselage explodes, this toy plane will be a jack-in-the-box."

I'd never told Devon, but my aversion to surprises stemmed from some pretty ugly incidents as a child confronted with that simple evil toy.

"Just a short ride, Pip. It's fine."

I didn't realize the clown behind me was listening until she spoke up.

"Don't worry, sweetie, we charter this flight whenever we go to Nebraska. The airlines stopped flying from Denver to Grand Island, and we're glad to have the company. Extra weight, ya know?"

That sure made me feel better.

"Well, glad to be of service in the extra weight category, and we do appreciate the ride. I hope you don't find me rude, but I'm a ball of nerves." I really felt terrible for making jokes at the clowns' expense. They were doing us a big favor. So, I squeezed my eyes shut and gripped the armrests so tightly my hands would be bruised for a month. Then I sent up a prayer to the flying circus gods.

"I'm so sorry, but we have nothing available. Call it rental car madness." The tiny little bee behind the counter buzzed with enthusiasm—and she flirted horribly with Devon and Simon. Who clearly flirted back.

"Listen, darlin'," Simon drawled. "We've got to get to that show. My sister and her friend here are backup singers, and we promised to have them there. You know how that goes, don't you?"

Dani and I looked at each other. With her coloring, she had to be the sister. No way did my pale skin and red hair match Simon's darker skin tone. She grabbed Simon's arm and squeezed it, probably tighter than necessary.

"Simon, you promised." She pouted for good measure.

"Tell you what. My brother has a car lot down the road. Shady Deals. Right over on Shady Bend. I'm sure he can find you something. Maybe George can give you a ride down there. He's a rideshare driver," the assistant said, pointing to the car out front.

Simon grinned and winked at her. "I sure as sugar appreciate that"—he looked at her name badge—"Carla. And if you manage to get over to the show later, look me up." With that, he took the map she'd circled the car lot on, and we strode out.

"Sure as sugar?" Devon laughed so hard tears streamed down his face. I had never seen the boys in action, not like that anyway, and they weren't even close to being done with that act. They kept it up as they negotiated with Carla's brother for a virtually new SUV.

"Why are they buying a car?" Dani whispered as we hung back and watched.

"Because evidently, they can," I whispered back.

When they came back out, keys and paperwork in hand, we headed over to the vehicle in question. I was about to burst with curiosity.

"How did you buy a car that fast? Nobody buys a car that fast?" I demanded, not that it stopped me from admiring the plush interior, complete with backseat consoles and temperature control.

"The price was too low not to, and it got even lower when I flashed my badge. Simon ran it, and it's not stolen, but it is highly suspect that some of the other vehicles in the lot are. We made him an offer he couldn't pass up."

"How much?" I asked.

"Not enough, and way too much," Simon said.

"Whose is it? Whose name went on the title? You did get the title, didn't you?"

That got me a sidelong look from Devon and a smirk. I shrugged and went back to examining the interior. If Devon bought it, I'd get to drive it, so it was all good.

Since there was plenty of time to kill before the show began, we decided to fortify ourselves, and as we entered the downtown area, we spotted the perfect place. Apparently, there was a genuine Coney Island hot dog shop in the middle of the corn belt, as in seriously good chili dogs, according to Yelp. So naturally, we had to stop. We parked down the block and across the street in front of what looked to be a historic building. The sign said it dated from 1886. Grand Army of the Republic building. Interesting, of course, so I snapped a photo, but what got my attention was the one-eyed Siamese cat in the window. I swore he was trying to talk to me. He kept putting up one paw to stop me every time I moved. So, I dubbed him Spook as I walked away while and mentally promising him I'd return.

After we'd each downed a dog, some truly fabulously greasy

French fries, and an old-fashioned coke—meaning fountain style in a glass that actually said Coca-Cola on it, we were off to find the ladies.

CHAPTER THIRTY-TWO

 in the arena. It was general admission, which generally meant chaos, but the ladies were in front of the stage. I tried to calculate how they'd managed that. They had driven, and we'd flown. So how had they gotten here first? Did the Luxmobile suddenly have wings? Regardless, we certainly didn't end up down in front. We were all the way in the back, and since the lights were flashing, it meant the show was about to start.

The show was kind of fun. I was a fan of eighties music, and the tribute bands did a hell of a job. My favorite was the Go-Go's tribute. Dani and I danced and sang through that set while Simon and Devon kept a lookout. When the emcee came on stage and told everyone to get ready to rock it out with Jon Von Jobi, the crowd went nuts, and the boys disappeared. The intro music died out, then Trey Marks stood center stage, his gaze transfixed on the audience below. Specifically on Matilda McDonald.

Dani and I held our breath, and murmurs started in the crowd. Then Matilda shouted, "Run, Trey. Run..."

He turned and looked behind him, dropped his mic, and

ran. Matilda suddenly sprinted off to the side of the stage with her BFFs in tow, leaving the emcee fumbling with the mic and trying to gain control of the situation. Devon and Simon were nowhere to be seen. It was total chaos.

I looked at Dani and shrugged. "Shall we?"

"We shall."

She grabbed my hand as we made our way down the steps to the floor, barreling through the crowd. Dani searched one side, and I took the other. When the music started up again, Block of Blackbirds had taken the stage. People settled in, and we were able to squeeze our way to the front. I spotted the women off to the side. They saw us approach and quickly made a beeline for the exit. We caught up with them outside as they raced toward the RV. My mother suddenly stopped and put up one hand while Prudence, Hope, Marcy, Matilda, and Rosa scurried up the RV steps.

"Privacy, girls, we need our privacy. Regardless of how you got here, you can leave the way you came."

With that, she hopped aboard the beast and burned rubber.

I shook my head. "Well, that was rude."

"We'll have to find Simon and Devon," Dani said.

"I'm pretty sure they've caught up with Trey, which was why the women were so angry. Devon probably cuffed him and hauled him off somewhere." I couldn't blame Devon, all things considered. If Trey were a raving homicidal maniac, shared DNA or not, Devon wouldn't want him anywhere near Matilda.

Dani and I headed to where we'd parked, hoping the SUV was still there. We didn't have the keys but spotting the vehicle would guarantee not everyone had ditched us. Yet. Then my phone buzzed.

Devon: You and Dani take SUV and head home. Keys in your bag of fun.

Me: Seriously?

Devon: Most definitely.

I reached into my purse and pulled out a set of keys I hadn't put there.

"Road trip. I wonder if we can stay for the end of the show?"

Dani laughed. "Which one?"

In the end, we decided it would be better if we left. We were just getting into the car when someone shouted behind us. I turned. Simon and Devon raced across the parking lot.

"Hold the fort and throw me the keys, babe." Devon was breathing hard, but certainly not as much as me if I'd run the distance between the building and the SUV.

"You didn't just call me babe. I thought we'd established you were never to call me babe." I threw him the keys along with a look that hopefully delivered my message.

"Sorry, Red." He hopped into the driver's seat and started the car. Simon took shotgun, and Dani and I, once again, ended up in the back.

As we peeled out of the parking lot, I tapped Devon on the shoulder. "Hey, lead foot, what's going on? Why are we in such a hurry, and where are we going?" I had assumed Devon and Simon had arrested Trey. Handing him over to the local authorities didn't seem likely. So where was he? Then I suddenly had a lightbulb moment.

"Ooooh."

"Yeah, ooooh is right," Devon said. "We don't have him. They do."

"Perhaps you'd better explain."

"There isn't a lot to tell," Simon said. "We spotted him heading out a side exit, but as soon as we followed him, he'd disappeared. When I looked toward the RV parking lot, I saw someone dodging in and out and, assuming it was him, ran over there. Then Devon's phone rang."

"Yeah, it was my mom asking where I was and if I would meet her inside." Devon sighed.

"She tricked you," I said, pointing out the obvious.

"I prefer to think she manipulated me."

"The queen rules again," I remarked. "Assuming they have Trey on board, why don't you call her and tell her to pull over? Or better yet, have the cops pull them over for speeding."

"Because she's my mother, and, biologically speaking, he's my father."

"Then what's the plan?" Dani asked. "Chase them back to Luckland?"

"No need to chase them. We've got a foolproof plan," Devon replied. "Isn't that right, Simon?"

"As always, Dev. As always."

I was not convinced. When it came to the Luckland Ladies, nothing was foolproof.

CHAPTER THIRTY-THREE

My phone buzzed. It was my mother. To read the text or not to read, that was the question. I read it.

Mom: Tell your boyfriend to release his hostage imme-diately.

Wait, what? They didn't have him? Uh-oh.

Me: What hostage? You're the ones with the fugitive.

I spoke as I typed so everyone knew what was going on.

Devon immediately flipped on his signal and pulled off the highway, coming to a stop on the side of the service road.

"What the hell is going on?" he demanded. "They don't have him? That can't be."

Simon shook his head. "We don't have him. They don't have him. So, where's our homicidal crooner?"

"Cut it out, Simon. We don't know he's an actual crooner," Devon replied.

"They could be lying," I said. "I wouldn't put it past them."

"Might I make a suggestion? Maybe he was hiding out in the men's room," Dani said. "That's what they do in the movies."

Simon and Devon shared a glance. Not the condescending

kind either. The rueful, sheepish kind. As in, they hadn't even considered it.

Simon stepped out of the car, which seemed a bit dangerous, seeing as we were on the side of the road and in the dark, but he appeared to be making a phone call. I guessed he was contacting his sources to pick up Trey in Grand Island. I was pleased with how this was turning out. If Trey proved not to be a murderer, I wanted to be there when Matilda and Trey reunited. If they'd been in the RV, I'd have clearly missed out on a truly romantic moment. Of course, if Trey *had* killed Tony…

Simon got back in the car and nodded at Devon, who pulled out and veered back onto the highway. Onward we went, homeward bound.

We finally pulled into my driveway in the wee hours of the morning. Dani and I wasted no time getting out of the car. Stretching and yawning, we headed right inside and up the stairs. I was in desperate need of my comforter and pillow.

***

Morning came too quickly. Before I could even summon the strength to open one eye, my furry friend busily pawed at my face. Sometimes, she thought my cheeks were catnip. I batted her away only to have Devon replace her, not pawing but playing prince charming, trying to kiss me awake. Worked every time. I dutifully got out of bed, threw on a pair of yoga pants and a t-shirt, and headed down for coffee—which was when I realized it was still dark out. Not yet time for human awakenings. Plus, that was when I remembered the date.

"Dev, we are now town pariahs," I said somewhat sadly.

He looked at me quizzically. "What do you mean?"

"We didn't leave candy for the trick-or-treaters last night for Halloween. This means we will never see trick-or-treaters at our doorstep ever again." I felt really horrible about that. The spooky holiday had seemed to flit by with all the other mystic mayhem going on.

"Fear not, Glinda. I took care of it."

Now that was a surprise. "Do tell."

"I noticed the jumbo bag of candy you'd purchased, and I was going to surprise you." He grinned at that. "I bought one of those big bowls with the creepy hand that pops out when you reach in, filled it, and had it hidden. Then, before we left yesterday, I put it on the porch. You walked right by it when you went in last night. You were so tired you didn't notice it."

I wasn't sure how I missed that, but I was glad I did. The bowl probably would have been ten times worse than a jack-in-the-box.

Simon entered the kitchen then, shirtless once again. I smiled. Nothing like eye candy in the morning.

"Good morning, Pippa, Devon," he said quite cheerfully.

"Well, you're certainly in a happy mood. For a guy who lost a homicidal crooner yesterday," I said.

"Simon, please tell Pippa where we're off to this morning—once you've had the decency to clothe yourself," Devon said with a cheeky grin.

"That ramshackle house of yours." Simon poured himself a mug full of caffeine.

"Please explain why?" I asked.

"Because Trey is there."

"Trey is where?" Dani asked as she came into the kitchen. "Where are we going?"

"Mystic Manor. The boys think Trey is there. Wait, what?" Still a bit foggy, I'd just realized what they'd said.

"Okay, so a few things you should know," Devon said. "State troopers picked up Trey at a truck stop in Western Nebraska, and Simon and I might have slipped away while you were sleeping to participate in that effort. Then we took custody of him and brought him to the Manor."

"What? You're saying you guys made a run in the middle of the night to fetch a criminal?"

Simon nodded. "Well, yes, but they met us halfway."

That information didn't explain why the state troopers would hand a suspect over to a Luckland police department of one. Then I remembered Simon was FBI. So maybe that was why.

"Why the Manor? Why didn't you take him to your office?"

"We'll explain when we get there. Actually, we'll probably let Trey explain."

They had to be a few marbles short, but I was willing to go along with their harebrained scheme. After one more cup of coffee.

As it was a nice morning, albeit a bit brisk, we decided to walk to the Manor, which, aside from Billy poking his little head through the fence, appeared deserted. I could see he obviously missed my presence, so I immediately went over to pet him. He was quite adorable. Simon seemed to hang back, not wanting to get too close, which amused Dani to no end.

Once I'd properly greeted Billy, another snort reached me. Not Billy. Turning, I realized Doc Stormy had delivered on his promise. Nudging Billy out of the way, our new resident poked her nose through the fence. Giving her head a few rubs, I realized she looked just like Billy, except her ears were a lovely bluish-gray color.

"Hello, little one. I shall dub you Skye."

"Don't I get to help pick out a name?" Devon asked.

"Nope, now onward, Dr. Doolittle." I didn't want to wait a minute longer to meet our guest.

CHAPTER THIRTY-FOUR

I HAD NO IDEA WHAT TO EXPECT WHEN WE ENTERED THE HOUSE. Certainly not to find Trey Marks, aka Jon Von Jobi, sitting at the ad-hoc kitchen table, which was nothing more than a card table. Trey appeared to be enjoying coffee and donuts. What a coincidence.

He looked up as we entered and flashed a grin. My heart flipped over several times. Sitting in front of me was Devon Marks's father—no DNA needed. They were the spitting image of each other. Did Trey realize who he was to Devon? I had a funny feeling he didn't.

"Simon. Devon. Nice to see you again, and thank you for these donuts, which are fabulous by the way," he said. "And who are these two gorgeous girls?" Trey winked, then lifted his mug and leaned back in his chair precisely the way Devon did. How was that possible? I'd heard of the phenomenon. Particularly among siblings raised separately. But just...*wow*.

"This is Pippa and Dani," Devon replied. "Pippa and I are... Well..." He looked at me for help. I tipped my head and smiled. This one was on him.

Trey chuckled. "I get it. No need to explain."

"You're the singer who caused quite a stir from last night's concert," I said, impatient to find out what he was doing here but not wanting to let him know I knew his identity.

"Oh, you were there too?"

"I was, yes. So, what caused you to run off the stage like that?"

Trey looked at Devon, who nodded.

"Well, it's a bit of a strange tale and a tad long. You might want to have a seat." He chuckled as he pointed to a couple of chairs. "Where to begin? Well, a few days ago, we were down in Tucson for a gig. I sing mostly tribute stuff. Jon Von Jobi? You might have heard of me. Anyway, there I was, getting ready on the tour bus, doing my thing, singing in the shower. Just warmin' up, you know. I heard a noise, so I stepped out, dripping wet, mind you, and there's this goon standing there. First thing he does is sucker punch me." He paused, took a sip of coffee, and shook his head as if confused. "He started asking about someplace called Luckland. Said if I didn't tell him what he needed to know about the gold, they would *take out* my son. I was thinking, I don't have a son, I've never been to Luckland, and I definitely didn't know about any gold. I wasn't sure what they were after, and truthfully, I didn't care. I just grabbed the nearest thing I could find. I think it was a flashlight. It was good and heavy, so I swung it. It hit him in the face, and he fell. Scared he might have had a partner, I grabbed my bag and took off. After a while, I heard sirens, saw the commotion, and decided it would be best to disappear."

Expression remorseful, he looked at Devon. "I probably shouldn't have left, I know that now, but nothing like that has ever happened to me. Anyway, I decided to make my way to the next stop on the tour. I mean, I didn't know the guy was dead or I was a wanted man, let me tell you."

He sighed, then smiled softly. "Then there I was on stage,

about to lay into my first number, when I saw the woman I've dreamed about for thirty years. My one and only love. She was right down in the front. Tillie. My Tillie. I was floored. I was going to jump right off that stage when she shouted for me to run. The look on her face. It went from joy and love to sheer panic. I turned, saw these two in the wings"—he nodded at Devon and Simon—"and self-preservation kicked in. I thought they were another couple of goons, you know? So, I ran. Went out the back way, got in my car, and took off. Then the troopers pulled me over and cuffed me. Can you imagine? They took me down to their office, quite excited about it, as if they'd snagged the FBI's most wanted. Me. Unbelievable. I've never even had so much as a speeding ticket. Well, maybe once. But I was more worried about Tillie. I had no idea why she tried to warn me or how she figured thugs were chasing me, but I kind of hoped she'd hear about my arrest and come find me." He looked at Dani and me and smiled broadly.

"Here's the good part. Just when I thought I was in some serious sh—eh, stuff, an officer came in and told me he was moving me someplace else. I followed him right out of the station and into a waiting car, and we drove about an hour, stopping at a truck stop for coffee. Then in walk Devon and Simon. I still had no idea what was happening, but they convinced me they weren't there to harm me. Then I rode with them here to Luckland and explained the whole thing all over again. Only this time, they seemed to believe me. Those other guys didn't."

"We do believe you, and we certainly understand how confusing this must be for you," Devon said quietly.

"It is. But I really only have one question. Perhaps you can tell me where my Tillie is? Help me find her?" He looked so hopeful I wanted to grab him by the hand and drag him over to her house, but Devon shook his head slightly in warning.

"Perhaps we can. Do you recognize this photo?" Simon laid a photocopied picture of Trey and Matilda on the table.

Trey's facial expression went from curious to stunned. After a moment, he gently lifted the photo and lightly brushed across the image of Matilda. He looked up and shook his head in wonder. "Tillie," he whispered. "This was a long time ago."

"This was found in the pocket of the man who attacked you," Simon said.

Trey frowned, then looked at me. Maybe he thought I could help.

"Why? Is she in danger? We have to find her." His voice became louder as he spoke.

"She's safe at the moment," Devon said, his voice tight. He stepped forward and held out another photo, this time of Matilda and him as a baby.

Trey took the photo and studied it. He smiled—a sad smile if there was such a thing. Then he frowned. "A son. The man who attacked me said he'd take out my son. This is him, isn't it?" He looked at Devon for confirmation.

Devon nodded. "Me," he said quietly, his expression tense.

Dani and I slipped over to Simon, and the three of us quietly exited the room. It wasn't right for us to be there. This moment was Devon and Trey's, and theirs alone.

CHAPTER THIRTY-FIVE

WE HEADED BACK HOME, SAT IN THE KITCHEN, AND TALKED ABOUT what Devon and Trey were discussing. As much as we all understood their need for privacy, we also really wanted to be a fly on the wall. I couldn't imagine what would be going through Devon's mind. It was one thing for him to know his father existed and another to sit in front of him.

When Devon came home a few hours later, he was alone.

"Where's Trey?"

"Luckland Inn. With instructions *not* to leave his room until I come for him." Devon pulled out a chair, then turned it around so he could sit and lean his arms on the back.

"What if he does leave? What if he's seen? Your mom will have a heart attack," I said.

"He promised, and I believe him. I reminded him we still had to see the Tucson police to sort out what happened down there, and if he left the room, I wouldn't vouch for him."

A tad harsh, but I could understand he had to be a policeman first, a son second. "Okay, so what else did you talk about?"

"Well, remember that photo of my mom at that concert?"

When Simon clearly had no clue, Devon pulled the now well-worn folded-up paper out of his pocket and handed it to Simon.

"Trey said he remembers her being there. Said he ran off the stage after his set to find her, they locked eyes, and just as he headed in her direction, some groupie stopped him. When he looked back up, Matilda was gone."

I thought about it and nodded. "I can see that. She probably misunderstood what was going on and was hurt by it. Probably ran off to lick her wounds."

Devon scoffed at that. "My mother would not have run off. She'd have told him off."

"No, Mr. Sensitivity, she wouldn't," I said. At Devon's confusion, I sighed. "Never mind. I assume you have a plan to get them back together?"

Devon grinned. "Karaoke night. Tonight."

Karaoke night at Matilda's was a long-standing tradition, mainly because Matilda loved to sing. She was actually quite good, but tonight was destined to be a night like no other. I was nervous for Trey, nervous for Matilda, and nervous that somehow something would go terribly wrong.

Dani and I headed over there early to find Matilda locked in her room, refusing to come out—still reeling from the shock of the previous night's events. Devon hadn't told the posse that Trey was in town. Only Simon, Dani, and I knew.

So, I needed to find a way to lure Matilda out without spoiling the surprise. I enlisted Dani's help, and we asked the ladies to give us a minute with Matilda. Alone. Matilda's maternal instincts would never allow her to refuse such a request. I hoped she'd think we needed advice or something.

We gently knocked before entering her room to find her

sitting on the side of her bed, head down and staring at a photo. Dani sat on one side of Matilda while I took the other. We looked down at the picture. It was one of her and Trey on a sidewalk in Vegas. I had to admit I'd never seen two people who looked happier. They were in a half embrace, just looking at each other. His hands were on her waist, and her hands were on his shoulders. I wasn't sure who took the photo, one of the ladies, probably, but if ever there was a photo that simply said *love* in its purest form, that was it.

"You were quite something," I said softly.

"We were, Pip. Best time of my life." She shook her head. "Had I known he was the one, had I not been so stupid..." She looked up then, her eyes red and puffy. "I'd never have left. You know, I did look for him. I went to a concert, and there he was. I thought he saw me. I thought it was going to be our moment. Instead, he ended up with some leggy blonde wrapped around him as if she was a tortilla and he was the filling. With my pride hurt, I left. It was only later I realized I should have stayed and tried to talk to him. When the girls told me they'd tracked him down and I would get a chance to see him, I was delighted. Now it's too late. He's on the run from the law, and I may never see him or talk to him again."

I glanced at Dani, who looked ready to burst at the seams. We wanted to put Matilda out of her misery and tell her Trey was only a few hundred yards down the road, but we'd promised not to say a word.

"Don't let that worry you, Tillie. Up you go, it's time you celebrated who you are and what you *do* have." Dani was in full-blown sisterhood mode. "I read that Ms. Helen Reddy passed away. I think you need to blow off some steam. What say we do a tribute to her."

That brought out a smile, albeit a tiny one. Matilda stood, and Dani led her over to her vanity desk and began to work a little magic on her eyes while I grabbed the red minidress from her closet.

"Really, Pippa. The red dress?" Matilda looked confused.

"Can't sing *I Am Woman* without it!"

Before long, Matilda was dressed to kill and ready to enter the world again. I could only hope she'd remain in that frame of mind until Simon and Devon pulled off whatever stunt they'd planned.

We'd created a monster.

Forty-five minutes later, she still belted out tunes. We'd heard about every woman's anthem ever recorded, and since we were outside on Matilda's multi-level deck, the whole neighborhood heard them. Devon stood next to me, watching expectantly. He still hadn't revealed his plan, and I was practically on the edge of my seat in anticipation.

When the music stopped, we all applauded, and I assumed Matilda would start out with another song.

"Is it my turn?" A deep voice came over the speaker system as Trey came up the steps to the main deck. The music started up again, and Matilda turned and came face to face with the love of her life as he began singing Bon Jovi's *Always*. Her expression was priceless.

"Son of a bitch. Would you look at that," Devon whispered with a grin.

As the song ended, I realized I was holding my breath. I slowly exhaled and waited. The atmosphere around the deck was surreal. Nobody spoke. Nobody moved. Trey fixed his gaze on Matilda, then dropped the mic and cupped her face in his hands.

"Tillie?"

"Trey?"

I'd never witnessed such a magical and romantic moment. I looked around for Devon, but it seemed he'd left. I texted him just to be sure.

Me: Where are you?

Nothing. Probably in his car.

I didn't know what to do next. My mom seemed to because she quietly moved about, telling everyone they ought to go home, leaving Tillie and Trey standing there. Babs still looked stunned, but Tom quickly ushered her away. I sighed, grabbed Dani, and we headed out front to find Devon, who sat in the car tapping his fingers on the wheel. We got in, waited for Simon, then headed home in silence.

"We're gonna give you guys some privacy," Dani blurted the minute we entered the house. She pulled Simon toward the staircase. His smirk indicated he didn't mind a bit.

What Devon had done for his mother was extraordinary. I detoured to the kitchen and poured a small glass of wine. Okay, maybe small was relative. I needed fortification.

I found Devon sprawled on the couch, head propped under his hands on the armrest. I debated whether to sit elsewhere or with him. With him. I slipped off my heels, listened for wayward guests, then went over to sit in the minimal amount of remaining cushion. It wasn't a big sofa, but we could squeeze in. He immediately made room and laid his head on my lap.

I leaned down and gave him a kiss. Maybe two. A few. Until he smiled. Once I had that, I knew he could take it from there.

"Do you want to know what happened after you left?" I asked.

"Affirmative, Red."

"Okay, so Trey says 'Tillie?' and she says 'Trey?'. Then they just stared at each other. After that, the posse basically shoved everyone out the door."

"That's it?" He looked disappointed.

"Well, I couldn't very well hang around and eavesdrop, Devon. Matilda and Trey needed time alone together. Isn't that why you left?"

"I don't know. I didn't think I should stay. I can't explain it."

"Do you think they'll work this out? Do you think he'll stay? Do you like him?" I had a lot of questions. I probably should have eased up, but he didn't seem to mind. He twirled a lock of my hair in one hand and slid his fingers up and down my arm with the other. I took that as a sign he was going to talk. Instead, he was out like a light in about a minute.

CHAPTER THIRTY-SIX

The familiar voice followed the ring of the doorbell and several raps on the door.

"Why is my mother banging on the door," Devon mumbled into my ear.

"Because it's your mother. Go answer it," I mumbled right back, though neither of us moved. With my arm cozily wrapped around his chest, I was way too comfortable.

Devon had eventually awoken from his nap on the couch, and we'd made our way upstairs, where we collapsed into bed as if we hadn't slept in weeks.

Finally, he extricated himself and threw on a pair of jeans—at least, I hoped he did, and he went down to greet his mother. I followed soon after and arrived to find Matilda and Trey in our kitchen, beaming like teenagers.

"Well, good morning, Pip. I'm so glad you're awake. We have news," Matilda said.

"Of course you do. Do we have coffee?" I looked out from under half-closed eyes at Devon, who handed me my mug.

I took a few precious sips, then sat down at the table and took a few more. "Okay, now I'm ready. News."

Devon grinned and sat next to me. "Ready."

Matilda and Trey looked at each other for a long moment. Then she turned back to us.

"I'd introduce you, but Trey says you've already met and had your talk, so now we can move on from all that." Nothing like brushing aside a thirty-year secret, but okay.

"We've been talking all night. Well, not all night." She smiled coyly. "I want to make sure you are fine with all this, Devon."

"All what? You haven't said."

"Trey is moving to Luckland. To be with me."

"If that's all right with you," Trey said.

"We cannot be apart any longer. We wasted so many years," Matilda said as she gazed at Trey.

"Your mother and I agree it's what's best. At least we can give this a try. With your blessing, of course."

Devon looked from Matilda to Trey and back again. I thought it was to assure himself more than anything. Then he nodded. How odd to hear Trey say, "Your mother and I," as if they were normal parents.

"I'm good with that. I'm happy for you. That you found each other." Devon sounded sincere, but I noticed a hint of something in his voice I couldn't place.

"And I found you," Trey said.

Devon relaxed. That was what he feared—his place in all this. I took that as my cue to leave. The three of them needed some privacy.

"I'm just going upstairs to change and let you all chat a bit," I said with what I hoped was a breezy tone. I didn't want them to think I'd linger at the top of the stairs, eavesdropping. It did occur to me though.

As it turned out, they chatted for a good long while. I didn't want to interrupt, nor did Dani or Simon, so we eventually left the house and headed to the café—which ended up being a good thing. The minute we walked in, I sensed something was off. Morgan stood behind the counter, arms crossed and scowling. Finn sat at a counter bar stool with a similar expression.

Prudence and Martin were seated in a corner booth, so I headed that way with Dani and Simon close behind. With the booth big enough for all of us, we had no qualms about joining them.

"Morning, Deputy. Now, Pru, tell me everything. What happened after we left last night? I know you know."

"Where are the lovebirds?" she asked first.

"With Devon, having a family reunion. We felt they needed some alone time. We probably don't have long, so spill it. We're all dying to know what happened."

"Oh, Pip, it's not my story to tell. I mean, it was terribly romantic, of course, but I really shouldn't be telling you. You were there when he dropped his mic and held her face as if it were porcelain. Then he scooped her up as if she were a tiny little bird. He swung her around and kissed her like, oh, I don't know... Like in *An Officer and a Gentleman*. That scene where Richard Gere gets the girl? Or more like *When Harry Met Sally* on New Year's Eve."

I couldn't remember seeing either of those movies, but I got the gist. "Like *Bridget Jones*? Kissing in the snow, romantic?"

"Oh yes, that's it precisely." Prudence sighed and smiled. "Then they broke apart and stared at each other again. Tillie started to cry, but Trey just brushed her tears away."

Dani frowned. "Wait. Did you see all that? I thought you'd left like the rest of us. Kate ushered us out as if we were piranha."

"We intended to leave, but, um, we might have hung around in the kitchen."

"And watched out the window?" I grinned. Those crafty women. I wish I'd stuck around.

"Yes, we did. Then they came in and sat by the fireplace in the living room. Trey had grabbed the blanket from the recliner and laid it over them. It was just the sweetest thing. I might have taken a photo or two."

"Oooh, let me see."

"Later, Pip. I don't want to expose anyone."

I pondered that. "Then you left, right?"

"Well, not exactly, you see——" Pru looked up.

I followed her gaze and watched as my mother, Rosa, Hope, and Marcy marched in. They didn't see us at first as they were gabbing away, but once they did, they came barreling toward us. Marcy and Hope slid a few smaller tables over so we could all sit together. I hoped they weren't going to silence Prudence. The story was just getting good.

My mother glared at Pru. "Did you tell them, Pru?"

"Now, Kate. She promised she wouldn't," Rosa said.

"And I most certainly did not," Prudence responded.

"Tell us what? Why shouldn't we know?"

"Oh, for Paulette's sake," Hope said. "It's a matter of *who* tells you."

"Who's Paulette?" Simon asked, utterly confused.

Dani leaned into him. "She doesn't like the name Pete."

Simon looked at me, but I could only grin. The women had a few...idiosyncrasies nobody could explain.

I looked around the table, impatient for someone to talk. "Is anyone going to tell us?" I finally asked.

"Matilda will tell you when she gets here, Pippa. Be patient." My mother just *had* to add that last bit.

"Fine. I'll be patient." Total lie. "In the meantime, why do Morgan and Finn look as if they're ready for fight night?"

Hope shrugged. "I can answer that one. Finn found out Morgan and Hunter were up to no good, all that haunting of the Manor business, and wouldn't change shifts with her next Saturday. She wanted the night off to go to some concert, and Finn refused. He said he's going to the very same concert. I'm not here to play referee. They'll have to work it out themselves."

"Yeah, well, she should be locked up for what she did." I still didn't believe she and Hunter managed to rig the house for *all* the hauntings and whatnot, but even so, forcing the crew to leave in the middle of renovations was kind of a deal breaker for me as far as being civil to her went.

"She still might be, Pippa," Simon said. "One never knows."

"Don't tease her, Simon." Dani chuckled and shook her head. "You'll get her hopes up."

"Nobody's getting her hopes up but me," a familiar voice said from behind me, followed by two cold hands on my cheeks and a fabulous kiss.

I smiled up at him. "Hello, there. Fancy meeting you here."

"Better make room. Mom and Trey will be here in a moment." Devon was all smiles, and it gave me all kinds of warm fuzzies to see him so genuinely happy. Having someone else's happiness impact mine so strongly was new for me, and I'd only just begun to realize how different it was to be part of a couple rather than always centering things around myself.

Hope signaled Finn, who added another table, which turned into two once he saw Babs storming in with Tom and Leah. I had texted her on the way to the café, knowing she'd be furious if I hadn't. By then, we'd extended the table in the booth so far out it took up half the café. When the happy couple strode in, all focus turned to them, and the entire place went silent.

Matilda and Trey stood at the end of the table, beaming. I wondered which of them would tell the story. Even though we all thought we knew, allowing them this moment was important.

Matilda nodded at Trey, and they sat down, almost in sync, which was a little uncanny. It was as if they'd spent the last thirty years together rather than apart.

Trey glanced at everyone. "As you all probably know, Tillie and I have a history together." He looked at her and smiled. "One that had far too long a separation. Since we all haven't been formally introduced, I'll begin by saying my name is Trey Marks."

CHAPTER THIRTY-SEVEN

They told their tale in bits and pieces, finishing each other's sentences. I guessed Matilda hadn't told him the real reason why the ladies had left Vegas in such a hurry—the stolen money they'd found, but Trey seemed to accept whatever she'd said and was just happy to have her in his life again. They fit each other; anyone could see that. His eyes welled with tears when he came to the part about how Matilda had put his name on Devon's birth certificate. He laughed when Matilda explained how she'd made up a backstory that Devon's parents were missionaries kidnapped in the Congo and that she was his aunt, not his mother. It was touching how Matilda's voice cracked when she spoke about how she learned Devon knew the truth. They went back and forth, sharing their story with all of us.

I was a sucker for happy endings, and this one was too long in coming. They were going to get married, it seemed, right away, and while they ogled each other and shared some fairly steamy kisses, the women began loudly discussing the upcoming nuptials.

As happy as I was for Matilda and Trey, I was uncomfortable

with the direction they'd pushed the discussion. Mostly the part where they kept hinting at a double wedding. Yikes.

It was time for me to slip out of there, so I made a lame excuse about going for a hike and finishing my blog post.

As I left the café, Dani's voice filtered through the door. "There is no way she's gonna go for that."

I didn't want to imagine what "that" was.

I ended up taking a short hike, getting some beautiful shots of the brilliant orange and fiery red autumn leaves. On the way home, I passed by the Manor and saw Billy out by the fence, munching away. I stopped for a moment to say hello. He slobbered on my hand through the gate before hopping off around the back of the house. I decided to go inside for a moment and check on things. Even with all the hauntings going on, fake and otherwise, I didn't think it would be so bad in there.

When banging came from the back of the house, I paused, wondering if another ghost was going to show their presence, but by the occasional swear word, Devon caused the banging.

"What's happening, Toolman?" I asked as I headed in his direction.

"Don't come back here."

"Why not?"

"It's a surprise."

"Wrong answer." I laughed—first because he threatened to surprise me and second because he seemed out of sorts. As I stepped into what would be our kitchen, I gasped. "Is that what I think it is?"

"It is," he said as he turned to me and smiled. A devastating smile. His wicked smile. He lowered his head and placed his hand behind my neck to draw me up for what was nothing short of an extraordinary kiss. The kind of kiss that transmitted enough volts of electricity to light up the town. And then some.

"Thank you," I whispered softly in his ear before squeezing the life out of him. I looked down at his masterpiece. For a guy of few words, he nailed it. A tin plaque with hammered lettering:

Mystic Manor

Home Sweet Home

"Let's call it a night, Red, as we have no idea what on earth we'll wake up to tomorrow."

I smiled as he reached for my hand, savoring the connection we had. After watching how two souls could reconnect after so many years without missing a beat, I didn't want to miss a moment of my journey with Devon.

November flew by with Trey and Matilda floating about town rekindling their love. Hope and Marcy were all abuzz with their latest project—they'd purchased the Luckland Inn and the attached bakery and moved the café to where the bakery used to be. My mom and dad were back to being small-town antique dealers, and Prudence and Martin gave the local teenagers a run for their money at Luckland's version of lookout point.

Devon and I still had to find the missing shoeboxes and figure out who had threatened the ladies. Things took a turn for the worse when the Tucson police informed Devon that they never found any shoebox in Tony the Tiger's possessions, just a letter with information about Trey and Matilda. The letter told Tony to force Trey to admit where the gold was, and Tony would be handsomely rewarded. There was no name on the letter, just a phone number. When the Tucson police tried the number, it was no longer in service. So, whoever had the shoebox with Matilda's secrets had used them to find information about Luckland's gold. If they'd tried once, it stood to reason they would try again.

Another thing that worried me was the increase in ghostly sightings and the Luckland Ladies' more frequent "meetings." Again, something suspect was going on.

Regardless, Devon and I needed to live our lives. Mystic Manor's renovations were coming along swimmingly. In fact, we'd moved in and had decided to host Thanksgiving dinner. I had high hopes, figuring with Devon's culinary skills and my love of cranberries… What could possibly go wrong?

Then my phone buzzed.

Devon: Emergency. There's been an accident!

SNEAK PEEK AT THE NEXT LUCKLAND MYSTERY
STOLEN RECIPES AND A DEAD CHEF

The ladies take a culinary road trip, but it's the chef who's sliced and diced.

When Aunt Hilda turns up for Thanksgiving dinner, the Luckland Ladies set out on a culinary road trip to find a recipe thieving chef. Dragged along for the ride, Pippa suspects murder when the chef turns up dead. And Hilda is the prime suspect. Proving Hilda's innocence isn't so easy when the chef's wife has photos that prove Hilda's guilt.

A bevy of spirits and messages from the past offer clues that might clear Hilda's name. In Pippa and Devon's search for the real killer, four of the six missing shoeboxes turn up, but the ladies remain steadfast in their refusal to reveal their secrets, which Pippa is beginning to suspect may be linked to Luckland's legendary gold.

CHAPTER ONE

I glanced at the text, then at Billy, one of the pigmy goats we'd recently adopted, but before I could react, Devon sprinted into the yard, a look of horror on his face.

Devon Marks did not wear horror well. He was a finely honed, smoking-hot chief of police who happened to be my brave, never frightened by much, significant other.

"What happened?" My heart banged the inside of my ribs, and a tic in my right eye twitched. This year, as the proud new homeowners of Luckland's finest reno project, we were doing the honors of hosting Thanksgiving dinner, and the thought of something going wrong had my adrenaline pumping.

Instead of answering, he pointed to the house. Fearing someone had gotten hurt, I raced through the back door to find my mom and her besties, the infamous Luckland Ladies, or as I affectionately called them, the posse, standing in a circle and staring down at something, or someone, on the floor. My mother, Kate, fluttered like a fairy. Matilda, Devon's mom, stood calmly next to her. Prudence tried not to laugh while

Hope and Marcy, the only two who belonged in the kitchen, wore curious frowns.

If there was going to be a calamity on Thanksgiving, I should have known they would be involved—though they didn't usually start tipping the bottle till at least noon. Since my twin sister Babs hadn't yet arrived, who or what lay on the floor was anyone's guess.

Finally noticing me, they broke the circle and allowed me to peer in.

"Who did this?" I looked closely at each of the women. All five turned toward Devon, who stood in the doorway. I focused my attention on him.

"Devon, my culinary wonder, is this your doing?" I pointed to the floor where sat the unfortunate victim.

"I'm afraid so, Pip," he said as a blush crept into his cheeks.

"How?"

"I don't know. It was like someone had greased him up. I couldn't keep hold of him." He shook his head, quite contrite with his puppy dog face. I melted.

"It's okay. I had a premonition the other day something like this would happen. So, I bought a spare. It's in the fridge in the garage."

I, Pippa O'Leary, was nothing if not prepared. I'd had a hunch several days earlier that something would happen to our Thanksgiving bird, though I couldn't determine what. Devon was a wonder in the kitchen. Tom Turkey going splat on my kitchen floor was...strange. Maybe supernaturally strange. Or ladies strange.

While Devon hurried off to fetch the turkey's replacement, I acknowledged that trying to host Thanksgiving in a home still going through renovations was monstrously over-ambitious. We'd only just finished our kitchen remodel. Admitting defeat, I let out a shrill whistle to stop the women's chatter.

"Change of plans. I think we should prepare our feast else-where. There's some bad mojo in here." I looked at the women, knowing they'd agree.

Bad mojo was what they called the mystical happenings we'd recently all experienced in and around Luckland, specifi-cally in my house we'd named Mystic Manor. With other-worldly apparitions, odd noises, and spooky sightings, Luckland was living up to its legend. Well, at least one of them.

Matilda nodded. "Right you are, Pip. Ladies? Let's take this over to the Inn, shall we?" They set to work gathering up the bags and baskets of food they'd brought and hustled out our front door.

When Devon returned with the backup bird, I told him about the change in plans.

He sighed. "Sorry, Red, I know you really wanted to host Thanksgiving."

I smiled at what I now considered an endearment. Growing up, when he called me Red, I usually looked for the nearest projectile to toss his way. "Only because *you* wanted to. You haven't had Thanksgiving with the posse in over ten years."

Devon's recent return home was just the start of a whole lot of changes in our cozy little town, and our personal lives.

"I'm sure it hasn't changed, and you know why I couldn't attend celebration dinners. FBI remember? Crime doesn't take a holiday."

"You remember it that well?" I circled him, gently poking him every so often to make a point. "Who's bringing sweet potatoes?"

"Prudence. Spiked with a fifth of rum." He grinned, exposing the dimple on his right cheek.

"Green bean casserole?" I asked.

"Your mom. Always. She claims it's the easiest."

"Crescent rolls?"

"Mom, who will also make the creamed corn." He raised an eyebrow.

"Oh no, Dev, we don't bother with that anymore."

Devon's smile fell. "She always makes creamed corn."

"Well, the thing is, since you never made it home for the holidays, she quit making it."

Maybe I'd gone too far in teasing the poor man. He did love his creamed corn. I leaned up and kissed his wonderfully handsome face. "Don't worry, I know for a fact there'll be your fave on the table. So, what shall we bring? Aside from a turkey."

"A case of wine? Because there's no way in hell we'll survive without it." He grinned, gave me a wink, and put his arms around me. It was perfect timing for my phone to buzz.

"Incoming text?" he asked, curious.

I glanced at my phone, then sighed. "From Babs."

Emergency. Luckland Inn.

CHAPTER TWO

THERE WERE A THOUSAND OR MORE THINGS I MIGHT HAVE ENVISIONED Babs could have meant when she texted there was an emergency. However, when we pulled up in front of the Luckland Inn, the disaster that played out on the sidewalk was beyond anything I could have dreamed.

My fraternal twin sister was always put together. Neat as a pin with never a hair out of place. She could have been the poster girl for the perfect holiday hostess in her trim, white winter jumpsuit. However, with green goo oozing down her body, she now resembled the poster girl for Ghostbusters. I wasn't sure how to react. My devilish side craved a big grin, while my sisterhood side wanted to reach out and hug her.

Before I stepped out of the car, Devon put his hand on my arm.

"Easy, Red. We have no idea how this happened. No sense riling her up."

"Understood, Kemosabe, but if you'd had siblings, you'd understand the sacrifice I'm about to make."

One side of his mouth pulled up as he shook his head.

As I approached Babs, I stifled my snicker and put on my

sisterly face, all concern and empathy, though I wished to god I'd brought my camera so I could capture the moment of Babs O'Leary-Cornwall covered in...whatever that was. Normally, bad things happened to me, so it was a nice change not to be on the receiving end.

Just then, my mother came running out the door, towels in hand, muttering something about a Sylvester.

I glanced at Devon, who seemed just as bewildered as me. We turned as my mother began wiping the goo, which looked like Jell-O, off Babs. Mom's efforts didn't work very well as Babs's lovely white jumpsuit took on a distinctly lime-colored hue. The more Mom rubbed, the greener the jumpsuit got. All we needed were some cinnamon candies to sprinkle on Babs, and we'd have had a winter wonderland cupcake in front of us. It didn't help that my mom, all five feet two inches of her, wore some sort of harvest holiday apron and an orange jumpsuit eerily similar to my sister's. I suspected they'd gone shopping together, as they often did. Mom's blonde hair, neatly trimmed in a bob, peeked out from beneath a pinecone hat. Considering my mom had just left Mystic Manor a few minutes earlier, her clothing baffled me. I knew for sure she'd worn jeans and a sweatshirt in my kitchen when she tsked over the turkey because my mom in a sweatshirt was an event not to be over-looked or forgotten.

"Devon, I have a horrible suspicion the posse somehow knew they'd end up here." I kept my voice low, though I was sure neither my sister nor my mother paid any attention to us.

"Hmm" Devon pursed his lips, then began biting the inside of his cheek. A sure sign of contemplation. "Do you think they greased the turkey?"

"I don't know, but I wouldn't put it past them."

"Wouldn't put what past whom?" my mom asked.

I grinned. "Nothing. So, what happened to you, Babs?"

"Sylvester," she said as she gently cleansed her face with a washcloth my mom handed to her.

"Who is Sylvester?" Devon whispered to me.

"No clue," I whispered back. "Let's find out." I took his hand and pulled him along to the main door of the Luckland Inn—where we were stopped short by a furry. AKA a human in animal costume. Sylvester the Cat. One mystery solved.

Sylvester wasn't the only surprise. A large group milled about the lobby of the Inn—squirrels, rabbits, and a fox mingled together in perfect harmony. I'd heard about furries, but this was the first time I'd been up close and personal with them, and I wondered what they were doing here because the Inn was technically closed for renovation.

Hope and Marcy, owners of the Blue Sky Café, had recently purchased the Inn along with the attached bakery. They'd already moved the café to the bakery but were still working on a few updates to the Inn.

The previous owners had remodeled and modernized the rooms upstairs, so they no longer resembled a brothel—the Inn's original purpose when built sometime in the late eighteen hundreds, but the lobby was eerily authentic. The original floor needed a good sanding and staining, and the chandelier wouldn't have looked out of place in a haunted house, which the Inn was purported to be. There had been many rumored sightings over the years of the Scarlet Lady. I never quite figured out whether scarlet referred to the dress she wore or perhaps something more gruesome.

"Devon, Devon, over here!" Trey, Devon's biological dad, who'd gone MIA for thirty years or so but had recently rekindled his relationship with Devon's mom, called from the front desk. Devon headed over. He leaned on the desk and listened while Trey waved his arms and pointed here and there as he spoke. Devon nodded, then indicated I should approach.

I leaned up against the desk and mimicked Devon's posture. "So, what's happening in here? Other than green goo disasters and a woodland creature's conference?"

"Oh, Pippa, I'm afraid this is all my fault. Tillie asked me to mind the desk last week while she ran off with the girls somewhere. The phone rang. I answered it just as she instructed. You know, 'Luckland Inn, can I help you?'" Trey shook his head and swallowed hard. "The woman on the phone, at least I think she was a woman, said they needed rooms to ring in the holidays. I assumed that meant Christmas or New Year's."

"Of course, Trey, anyone would," Devon said to reassure him.

"When she said the twenty-fifth, I assumed she meant December. You know, Christmas. Turns out, she meant Thanksgiving."

Understanding dawned on me. "They've booked a few days, and now they're here."

"Yes, yes, and so we have no choice. I guess we have extra guests for dinner. And only one turkey."

"Aren't they vegan?" I turned to look at the impromptu guests. "Why don't we add some vegetable and pasta casseroles."

Trey shook his head. "No, not vegan at all. In fact, when they got here, and I realized I'd misunderstood, they made it clear they were looking forward to a real feast. These folks don't have anywhere to celebrate, it seems, so they all get together with one another."

"You seem to know a lot about furries, Trey," Devon said, his tone curious.

"I've run into them now and again on the road. They're much like Trekkies and those who dress up at comic-cons. Same thing. Just a bit of cosplay."

I found that interesting. I'd never put much thought into furry culture. Perhaps I needed to read up on them.

————

After Babs's slime fiasco, which had happened when Sylvester had accidentally knocked into her while she navigated the group of furries with her notorious green gelatin salad held high above her head, she'd gone home and changed. I saw her enter the lobby about an hour later with my brother-in-law Tom and my niece Leah, who wore antlers in honor of the unexpected guests. As requested by me, Babs had also brought in my spare camera from the ladies' huge RV parked in Prudence's driveway. As an outdoor photographer, I wasn't often caught ill-equipped, so I thanked her and promised to take photos of Leah as a memento of the celebration.

We set up the private party room for the furries, as the rest of us would be dining at the big wooden table in the formal dining room. As *luck* would have it, Hope and Marcy had several turkeys available—confirming my suspicion they'd planned to host Thanksgiving all along. The ladies were just humoring Devon and me when we offered to host the big feast. I didn't know how, but without a doubt, they'd buttered up that turkey when Devon was otherwise occupied. I made a mental note to ask about those *spare turkeys*.

I truly hoped the rest of the day would go off without a hitch. However, this was Luckland, where nothing was ever as it seemed, so there was a strong probability that "Turkey Day" would become one more of Luckland's legendary tall tales waiting to be told and retold every year.

After taking several photos of the furry crowd and my gorgeous three-year-old niece, I tucked my camera safely in the office, then offered to help in the kitchen.

"What can I do to help?" I asked Marcy, who seemed to be in charge.

"Chestnuts. For the stuffing. Just cook those up in the microwave, then peel and cut in quarters if you would."

I may not have been a culinary goddess, but I could manage simple tasks. I placed the chestnuts on a plate and put them in the microwave. While I waited for them to cook, I began to gather what I'd need to prepare them. Popping commenced, and I assumed the chestnuts must cook like popcorn. That would make them easy to peel.

"Pippa, you did score them, didn't you?" Marcy's voice came across higher pitched than usual.

"Score?"

"Oh my god! You didn't..."

I didn't know I was supposed to score the shells with an X so they didn't explode. The cacophony of chestnuts detonating inside the microwave brought a crowd of furries into the kitchen to see what was happening.

Marcy quickly shooed me out of the kitchen even though I offered to clean up the mess. Apparently, I was now persona non grata.

"Here, Pip, you do this," Hope said as she shoved a cardboard box in my hands. It was a big box, especially for tiny little Hope. She wore one of her signature pencil skirt and blazer outfits in a muted orange in honor of the holidays. Her hair, which she styled every morning, she'd arranged in one of her updos.

Inside the box were snow globes and what appeared to be a full set of *It's a Wonderful Life* holiday town figurines.

"Me?"

"Of course, we're going to need photos to promote the holidays here at the Inn."

"And you want me to decorate?"

"Don't be silly. We want you to photograph everything. You're the one with the creative eye. You'll know what will work in the photos, so you might as well put the holiday decor out where it works best."

That was basically her way of asking me to decorate and take photos without *asking*. Clever trick. I sighed and set the box down behind me at the desk.

"Anything else?" I muttered somewhat sarcastically toward her retreating form as she scurried away.

As I started unpacking the box, Finn, the newly anointed Inn manager after faithfully serving the Blue Sky Café for several years between archaeology expeditions, ran up to me, breathing heavily.

"Finn? What's up?"

He shook his phone in front of my face. I quickly grabbed the phone before I got banged on the nose with it.

A TikTok video. He was a big fan. Me, not so much. I humored him and played it. The footage showed a flashing neon holiday sign that read "The only good furry is a dead one" over blurry footage of a furry, possibly a polar bear, lying on its side in an alley. The problem, aside from the horrid message, was the alley in the video looked to be the one behind the Inn, as signified by the dumpster in the background—the one that said Blue Sky Café on it.

I grabbed my phone and fired off a text to Devon.

Me: Emergency. Alley. Dead polar bear.

THE LUCKLAND MYSTERY SERIES

Grande Dames and a Vegas Heist
Aliens and the Dearly Departed
Mislaid Love and Found Bodies
Stolen Recipes and a Dead Chef
Vengeful Spirits and a Lost Gold Mine

More to come!